BACK TO US

A Dare With Me Novel

J.H. CROIX

"Each time you happen to me all over again." - Edith Wharton, The Age of Innocence

Sign up for my newsletter for information on new releases & get a FREE copy of one of my books!

http://jhcroixauthor.com/subscribe/

Follow me!

jhcroix@jhcroix.com

https://amazon.com/author/jhcroix

https://www.bookbub.com/authors/j-h-croix

https://www.facebook.com/jhcroix

https://www.instagram.com/jhcroix/

Chapter One

NORA

"What the —?!"

My brain couldn't even finish firing off the thought as I felt an abrupt jolt in the small plane just as the wheels touched the gravel runway. The aircraft listed roughly to one side before grinding to a stop as I tried in vain to keep one of the wings from striking the well-placed boulder protecting the tiny building. Only in Alaska would an open shed with benches and shelving be referred to as an airport.

The plane's wing scratched loudly against the boulder as I finally managed to bring it to a complete stop.

"What the hell?" I muttered as I leaned my head back against the seat. That was my complete thought. A fat lot of good it would do about my situation.

After taking a moment to collect myself, I climbed out to check and discovered one of my landing tires had blown out. Hopping back into the plane, I tapped my radio on and called air control to let them know. The radio operator assured me they would get the message over to my brother Flynn so he could reschedule my remaining flight this afternoon.

Meanwhile, my situation wasn't great. All things considered, a blown-out tire was no big deal, but it left me stuck for the time being. I also needed to check on the plane's wing. Despite the annoyance of my situation, it was a beautiful day with the sun glittering on the waters of Kachemak Bay. I'd practically landed in a postcard.

Taking a deep breath, I turned everything off on the plane, running the standard post-flight inspection before climbing out and assessing my situation more thoroughly. This airport was nothing more than a supply pickup and drop-off way station for several nearby Alaskan communities. Literally, no one lived here. The only way to get here was by plane, boat, or backcountry vehicles.

I rechecked the tire, thinking it probably blew out from hitting a rock when I came down. Losing control on the landing had brought one of the plane's wings up close and personal with that boulder and left a deep dent in the wing as a souvenir.

"Dammit," I muttered.

A lone eagle screeched in reply, and I glanced up to see one flying nearby, its massive wingspan casting a shadow on the ground below.

I could deal with the tire, but the wing's damage meant I wouldn't be flying this plane back until that was repaired. I slipped my cell phone out of my pocket, wondering if I had any reception. Some stretches of Alaska were so sparsely populated that reception was a distant dream. This area was isolated. However, it was close to more populous areas, and there were cell towers scattered at the higher elevations.

I'd flown here plenty of times, but I couldn't remember if I'd ever checked for reception here before. As a pilot in my family's small flight business, we dropped off mail and supplies here on a regular schedule. Nearby areas used four-wheelers for pick up and transport, while the more remote areas required more distant ferrying by planes.

Maybe this seemed crazy if you weren't familiar with Alaska, but even the more remote areas of Alaska were busy in the sky whenever the weather was safe for flying. Between the proximity to more touristy areas and geographic convenience, it was much faster to get places by small plane in Alaska for areas off the main road system.

"Aha!" I exclaimed when I saw that I had not one but three whole bars for cell reception.

I immediately called the main number at Walker Adventures, the outdoor expedition resort I owned with my two brothers and my younger sister.

"Walker Adventures," Daphne, my brother's fiancée, answered cheerfully.

"Hey, Daphne, it's Nora."

"What's up? I thought you were in the air for most of today."

I quickly explained my situation.

"Ohhhh. Well then, that's a pain in the ass," she began matter-of-factly. "I'm sure they've already radioed Flynn. He stayed in town at the plane hangars to work on some engine issue. Everybody else is up in the air. What can we do?"

"I need you to look at the schedule on the laptop. It's the one I keep in the pantry."

Daphne's laugh was dry. "I know. You've told me that's a central location. I personally think a pantry is for storing food, but I'm flexible about that for your benefit." I could hear her footsteps crossing the floor. In another second, she asked, "Okay, what am I looking for?"

"Click the bottom so the toolbar comes up, and then hit the tab that says schedule."

"Got it. Okay, here's what it says."

She read off the schedule, and relief washed through me when I realized Gabriel wasn't conveniently close to me.

"I need you to call Flynn. Have him get ahold of Elias and tell him to come by here and pick me up. He's the closest and should be landing soon. He'll have plenty of time to hop over here and get me."

"Consider it done. You're okay with waiting?"

"Of course, I'm okay. I'm bored, but it's beautiful out this afternoon. I just hope it holds. The wind is supposed to pick up later this afternoon. I'll only have to wait about an hour, though, so it should be fine. Plus, there'll probably be some magazines in the airport."

"The airport?"

I laughed softly. "It's a shed with two benches and some shelving, but it counts as an airport. The magazines are probably ancient, but it'll help me pass the time. See you tonight."

"You got it, girl. Call me again if you need anything," Daphne replied.

I hung up, smiling to myself and thinking I needed to take Daphne with me on a supply run one of these days. Aside from taking people on guided flight expeditions to see wildlife and the stunning Alaskan wilderness, Walker Adventures also had contracts to deliver mail and supplies to different areas in the southern part of Alaska. Running the business with my siblings made for a kick-ass job, and I was never bored.

I quickly unloaded the supplies I'd brought over today—some mail and a few things from a local hardware store. There was one heavy pallet, and I decided to wait for Elias to get his help with it. I could've handled it myself, but a little help never hurt anyone. I discovered the magazine selection was older than expected. I walked out, angling toward a rocky ledge that sloped down to a beach with charcoal gray sand and a wide variety of rocks. The runway here ran parallel to the water.

Alaskan beaches had the best rocks, and I could always collect more. I clambered down the ledge and began walking along the water. The tide was out, and I leaned over to gently carry a few starfish into the shallows. A seal noticed me and followed my progress. There was also a raft of sea otters nearby. They were gathered together, some resting on their backs and others frolicking in the water. The wind picked up slightly, and I turned back after a little while, both of my pockets filled with pebbles and rocks. They were all kinds of rocks here, including lava that had formed into lightweight shapes, almost weightless in your palm. A bright red piece of lava was my best find of the day.

A short while later, I heard the distinct sound of a small plane engine approaching. "Yay!" I cheered to myself unless I was counting the eagle that screeched above again.

I was waiting by my plane when Elias came in for the landing. Unlike me, no last-minute gust of wind threw his landing angle off course. The aircraft lightly bounced a few times before he came to a smooth stop. I couldn't see his face due to the glare of the sun, but I waved and turned to walk to my plane and fetch my backpack.

A few moments later as I reached into the back of the plane, the hairs on the back of my neck stood. Without looking, I knew it wasn't Elias. Gabriel was here. Fuck my life.

I'd been studiously avoiding Gabriel for several months now. I prayed my instincts were wrong.

"Hey, Nora." Gabriel's low voice came over my shoulder, sending a jolt of electricity and the most inconvenient desire I'd ever experienced coursing through my body.

My instincts were spot-on, but then Gabriel was a magnetic force. Taking a deep breath, I marshaled all of my tattered composure and turned. "Hi." I refused to say his name.

His eyes met mine, and his gaze alone felt like fire on my skin. I ignored the feeling. "I thought Elias was coming to pick me up," I added.

"We switched up the schedule this afternoon."

"Why?" I practically barked at him.

The love of my life and the only man who'd ever really gotten to me shrugged. "Because we could."

I felt the tension in my face, and my lips tightened, but I refused to discuss this further. There was no point. Elias wasn't here, and my ex was. Actually, I didn't even know what Gabriel was to me. I guess my ex-friends-with-benefits or some other bullshit.

"Elias wanted to get back earlier to have dinner with Cammi," Gabriel added.

That detail felt like a twist of the knife buried in my heart. Not only did Gabriel not love me, but it seemed everyone around us was falling in love. My eldest brother, Flynn, who I'd *never* thought would fall for anyone, was freaking in love and so content with Daphne it was almost a joke. I was happy for him. I really, *really* was. Then there was Elias, who'd fallen in love with Cammi, the best barista in town. Even Diego, who wasn't as much of a surprise because he was such a softie, was in love. That left me, Gabriel, Tucker, and my younger brother, Grant. I found a minuscule amount of comfort in the fact that there were still more of us not paired up.

I absolutely did *not* need to dwell on this. I let my backpack slide off my shoulder. "Can you help me unload that last pallet?" I pointed at the open compartment on the small plane.

"Of course."

For a moment, we studied each other. My eyes soaked him in greedily. Because I'd been so carefully avoiding being alone with him, I'd hardly let myself look at him in the past few months. Whenever we were together, we were with our nosy friends and family. I loved all of them, and I didn't want any of them picking up on the tension simmering between us.

Gabriel's mossy green eyes searched mine, and I swallowed, willing myself to be numb to him. The sun glinted on his auburn hair, illuminating the flecks of gold in it. At the right angle, it looked like he had a freaking halo. I definitely knew he didn't.

He had strong features—cheekbones cut at clean angles and a strong jaw. Of course, because life felt incredibly unfair when it came to Gabriel, he had a smoking hot bod. He was tall with a rangy build, muscled shoulders, and arms that could make a girl weep.

My gaze dipped down, tracing over the way his T-shirt clung lovingly to his muscled chest. He had a hand in his pocket, and my eyes traced the flex of his forearm from where his thumb curled over the belt to his jeans. The distracted moment snapped when an eagle screeched again. That sound was followed by the chatter of a crow, probably trying to annoy the eagle. They were good at that.

Gabriel strode past me. "You get the other side," he said after he dragged the pallet halfway out of the back.

Within a few minutes, we had it inside against the far wall of the shed, protecting it from the elements if any weather came through. Deliveries here could wait a few hours, or even days, depending on the schedule for whomever planned to pick them up.

"Looks like your tire blew out," he commented as we walked back toward my plane.

"No shit," I muttered.

Gabriel glanced at me, his eyes narrowing. "You don't have to be angry every fucking time I'm near you, Nora."

"Maybe I don't have to, but I want to."

His nostrils flared before he let out a breath. Spinning away from me, he rounded the back of the plane to look at where the wing scraped against the boulder.

"Not bad. I can come back tomorrow with some supplies and patch it up," he commented as he returned to where I was waiting. His eyes skipped down to the blown-out landing tire and back up.

"You'll need someone to come with you."

"I assumed you would. This is your plane," he replied.

I suddenly felt crowded. I was between the door and the wing and felt hemmed in with Gabriel standing right there.

"It's not specifically *my* plane," I corrected.

My neck was hot, and my skin felt prickly all over. Longing pierced me, and I tried to shove it away, but I was helpless to my body's reaction to him.

"I know it's not yours, but it's the one you usually fly," he countered.

The moment fell quiet, silence spinning out between us. He stepped even closer, and I thought my entire body might go up in flames. Even worse, I didn't want him to move away. I wanted him—to the point of desperation.

Chapter Two

GABRIEL

A few hours earlier

"What?" I barked into my phone.

"I'm rerouting this afternoon to pick up Nora," my friend and fellow pilot, Elias, repeated.

"Is she okay?" Worry churned instantly in my gut.

"As far as I know. I'm sure they'd have mentioned if she wasn't." His tone was way too relaxed.

"Let's switch up our schedule," I said.

Elias chuckled, and I didn't even want to get into what he thought about my request. "Only if it means I get home earlier. When's your last flight?"

I quickly recited my schedule, adding, "Your only motivation is to see Cammi sooner, not help a friend out."

I could imagine my friend's amused shrug. "Maybe so, but I'd help you out anyway. It's just a bonus that I *will* get home earlier. On that note, I gotta roll, or I'll be late for your next flight that's now mine."

Hanging up, I immediately dialed my next call.

"Nora's at the supply stopover," Flynn, my friend and my boss explained a moment later. "One of the tires blew out on the landing gear when she landed, and she clipped a wing on a boulder. Look at her plane while you're there too, would ya?"

"Got it," I replied, trying to keep my tone level.

"Also, if you don't mind, could you give her a ride back home once you land on this side of the bay?"

"Sure." I gritted my teeth and took a slow breath. "Something wrong with her car?"

"Nah. She rode in with Grant this morning. He forgot, and he's already back out here."

"Of course. Catch you later."

Flynn hung up, and I let out a sigh. I wanted time alone with Nora more than just about anything. Yet if the past few months were any indication, I could count on her being radio silent. I was snatching this chance for some privacy with her, though, hoping maybe we could finally talk.

Worry spun like a whirling dervish in my thoughts, tightening in my chest. I'd fucked up with Nora worse than I could've imagined. I didn't know if I could ever repair the jagged tear between us. But I could definitely fix whatever was wrong with her plane. I didn't want to think about just how crazy I might've gone if she'd experienced anything other than a bumpy landing.

A few minutes later, I arrived at the airport in Diamond Creek, the one for small planes only. Two-seater planes dotted the Alaskan skies. Flying was a big business here, both for practical reasons and for tourists. I worked for Walker Adventures, owned by Flynn and his siblings. I still hoped my old friend didn't know just how bad I had it for his sister.

Flynn was one of my best friends, and we'd been in

the Air Force together. I had my reasons for telling Nora I could never commit. I just didn't count on my heart already being a lost cause.

An hour or so later, my eyes landed on the blown-open landing tire on her plane. My gut clenched, and I tried to breathe through the ache in my chest. I forced my eyes up, only to collide with hers.

Nora had her hand curled just inside the open door by the pilot seat. I stepped closer, moving on instinct.

"Are you okay?" My words came out abruptly, the edges sharp like the blades Nora had been dragging across my heart for the past few months.

She squared her shoulders, and I discovered I was closer to her than I meant to be. That was pretty much the story of my heart and Nora.

Her brown curls were mussed, and her matching rich brown eyes were snapping. "I'm fine," she bit out. "What the hell are you doing here?"

The sound of her voice felt like a bolt sliding into place inside me, but I forced myself to stay focused. "Flynn called me and said you had a problem with the landing. He wanted me to stop and check. Also, Grant forgot he needed to give you a ride home."

I knew I should've stepped back, but I couldn't bring myself to do so. The need to feel close to her, to soak in her presence ran so fierce that I couldn't override it with my brain.

Nora blinked, her mouth falling open before she snapped it shut. "I don't know why Flynn called you. I'm obviously fine. I can deal with it."

I rested my hand on the open door, curling my fingers around it. The cool metal barely broke through the fiery heat scorching me. The voltage snapped between us in a nearly electric connection. Once upon a time, as recently as a few months ago,

I'd convinced myself it was just desire and nothing more.

I was deeply aware of the folly of that thinking now. She'd taken it away—her touch, her laughter, her sweet lips against mine—but the grip she had on my heart hadn't loosened, not one increment.

"I'm sorry," I said finally, my words coming out raw and hoarse.

She blinked, and I saw the pain flash in her eyes. She shuttered it quickly, lifting her chin. "For what?" She threw that question at me like a dart.

"For telling you I didn't want more. For saying I could never commit."

My heart was pounding so hard, I could feel the hammering echo down to my bones. She stared back at me.

Because my body was always ahead of my brain and my heart when it came to Nora, I dipped my head, brushing my lips over hers. When I realized what I'd done, I braced myself, thinking she was going to shove me away and maybe even slap me.

She didn't. I felt the little whimper in her throat like a jolt of lightning through my entire system. And then, I was folding her in my arms, breathing in her scent—earthy with a hint of something sweet and overlaid with the crisp smell of the ocean breeze.

She still didn't shove me away, and I cataloged the feel of her pressed against me. She was already imprinted on every cell in my body—the sweet curve of her breasts against my chest and the dip of her waist where my palm landed. Her ragged breathing followed the rhythm of mine.

She let me hold her just long enough that hope unfurled in my heart like a banner across the sky with her name emblazoned on it. Then she stiffened. "I can't."

I forced myself to step back. The effort ran against every instinct clamoring in my body. Finally having Nora in my arms for the first time in months reminded me of just *exactly* how right it felt when we were together.

When I looked down, her brown eyes stared back at me. I thought I saw a teardrop glittering in her eyelashes, but a punishing gust of wind struck us, and her hair blew wild. By the time she brushed it away, the teardrop was gone.

"You know we're probably gonna have to stay here tonight, right?"

"What are you talking about?" Pink crested on her cheeks.

I waved vaguely in the air. "It's windy as hell." I gestured toward the wind sock on a pole mounted above the shed. As if to demonstrate, another brutal gust of wind lashed the poor wind sock, sending it into a furious spin before it held straight as the wind blew steadily.

"Unless the wind dies down real quick, we're not gonna have time to get back across the bay before it's too late."

Nora blinked at me before looking away, her chin set in a stubborn line. I knew she was grinding her teeth because I saw the muscle tightening at the back of her cheek. I wanted to pull her into my arms again and tell her I knew how much I'd screwed up. I didn't.

She slipped between me and the door, rounding to the other side of the plane and opening the small compartment in the plane's belly. A moment later, she closed it, slipping her arms into the bright purple windbreaker she'd pulled out.

"How long should we wait?" She stopped beside me, surprising me with her question.

Nora had been giving me the silent treatment for months now. It was crazy to realize how much I could miss her when she was right there. Every day. We worked together and lived at the resort together.

"Let's radio over to the other side of the bay and see how things look there."

I was surprised, yet again, when Nora followed me over to my plane. We climbed in the front. A moment later, Skylar Bridges, who ran one of the other flight businesses in Diamond Creek, answered, "Yep, what's up?"

I wasn't using the official channels for this call. I wanted a quick, preferably blunt answer. "How's the wind looking over there?"

"It's windy as hell," she replied.

Nora wrinkled her nose, her mouth twisting to the side. I chuckled. "Okay, so it sounds as bad over there as it is here at the supply station."

"It's probably worse over there because it's at a higher elevation. All of our planes are on the ground now. If you're smart, you'll sit tight. You set to stay for the night?"

I risked another glance at Nora. She was staring out the window to the side, but I could see the tension in her shoulders. My eyes shifted down to land on her hands, which were laced together tightly.

"I'm always prepared. It's summer, so it shouldn't be too bad as far as the temperature," I replied.

"Make sure to call in your flight update."

"Of course. Catch you later."

I ended that call and then went through the official channels to notify them that Nora and I would be remaining at the supply station until tomorrow morning. After I set down the radio receiver, silence fell around us.

Wind buffeted the plane, and my eyes lifted to see how the wind sock was faring, a simple yet effective indicator. It blew wild and twisted with another gust of wind. Trying to fly in wind like this was a fool's game.

"How are you doing as far as food goes?" I asked.

"I always have something on hand," she said quietly. "What about you?"

"Same."

She glanced at her watch, and as if on cue, my stomach rumbled. Her eyes flicked to mine, and then she laughed, just a little bit. My heart felt split open as swiftly as a log fell in two pieces with a single swing of an ax. That was how it was when it came to my heart and Nora. She had no idea. I hadn't even known it until I ruined the best thing I'd ever had.

"I even have a little camp stove," she offered.

I chuckled. "Of course you do."

"Why, of course?"

"Because you're always prepared. It's one of the things I like best about you."

"Let me see what I have. We can sit in the airport." She rolled her eyes at that. It was a running joke amongst the pilots who came out this way that the shed was actually referred to as an airport. "It'll keep us out of the wind."

A while later after we made sure both of the planes were situated for the night, Nora was sitting cross-legged on the floor in the shed. She had a lightweight portable propane camp stove set up and was presently preparing macaroni and cheese out of a box. I'd propped up a makeshift barrier in the doorway to keep the wind to a minimum. The wind hadn't eased up at all, and it was past eight o'clock. The sun was sliding down the sky, which we could see through the opening outside. It was a splashy sunset, the sky a swirl of reds, oranges, and golds. Darkness wouldn't come for more than another hour.

Nora was being polite to me, and being with her like this had my heart aching.

A few minutes later, she handed me a small plastic bowl with a spoon. "Dinner is served. It might not be as good as Daphne's cooking, but it'll do." We'd lucked out when Flynn fell in love with Daphne. She happened to be a kick-ass chef and now handled all the meals for the resort.

"It's better than my energy bar," I said with a chuckle.

I got a slight smile in return, which was remarkable. I took a few bites, then paused to sip water from a bottle. When I looked over at Nora and felt that now-familiar thread of tension between us, my heart lurched uncomfortably.

"I'm sorry." My words startled me. Not because I didn't mean them. I felt them down to my bones. As sorry as I was, I felt stuck, unsure how to repair the rip I'd torn in our relationship.

Nora's mouth fell open. She'd been in the process of lifting a spoonful of the pretty freaking good macaroni and cheese into her mouth. She'd added extra cheese from a few cheese sticks in her backpack, so it was nice and gooey and didn't have the distinct flavor of packaged food.

My heart thrashed in my chest in a messy, unsteady beat that echoed with thundering kicks.

Chapter Three

NORA

My hand was shaking, and I forced myself to lower it before I dropped the spoonful of macaroni and cheese all over my lap. My eyes stung, and I abruptly realized I might be about to cry. For the second time today.

I cried so much over Gabriel after he threw my feelings back in my face. I thought I had thoroughly and completely boarded up the windows, doors, and walls around my heart. I'd even built a moat, metaphorically speaking, but apparently, that wasn't enough to protect me, and I needed a freaking fortress.

Here I was, almost crying after he kissed me earlier, and now almost crying because he apologized. Jesus. I was pathetic.

"What?"

My mouth formed the word, but my lips felt almost numb. The rest of me felt raw, as if his mere presence had sliced me to ribbons.

"I'm sorry," he repeated.

I blinked at him, hoping I blinked the tears away. "For what?"

He set his bowl on the floor beside him. Leaning back against the bench, he stretched out his long legs with his feet crossed at his ankles. No matter what Gabriel did, he exuded a relaxed, easy masculinity. My eyes dropped down, drawn to the motion of his hand. He was tracing along one of the worn wooden floorboards in here. Lord knows when this place was built. The simple rectangular structure could've been here for decades. Somebody had replaced the roof at one point to a bright red steel, which made it easy to spot from the sky when you were flying over. The inside was completely unfinished—just plain wood benches and shelves, all of it covered in dust.

The sea-scoured wind blew inside, the air salty and dry as I waited for his reply.

"I'm sorry for screwing everything up," he finally said. "Can we try again?"

I stared at him blankly. My heart set up a raucous cheer while my mind scrambled to backpedal on that excitement. No need to let my heart get stupid all over again. Well before Gabriel broke my heart, I'd learned not to trust men. My father taught me well. Never trust a man to hang around. *Definitely* never trust a man to take care of your heart.

"Try what again?" I heard myself asking.

I wanted to smack those words right back into my mouth. Too late, they were already out there. I wished the wind would blow them away. No such luck.

Gabriel angled his head to the side, his eyes watching me quietly while my heart beat like a jackrabbit in my chest and butterflies twirled madly in my belly.

"Us," he said simply.

"Gabriel, we already did that. I can't do the whole

friends-with-benefits thing. I can't be your dirty secret. I just can't."

It hurt to say that, but it was all true. You see, I loved Gabriel. I fell in love with him not long after I fell into bed with him.

"I'm not asking you to be my dirty secret. Let's really do this."

"Do what?" I felt as if I had to keep clarifying every detail so there was no misunderstanding. Because the last time I misunderstood, it had nearly broken me.

He didn't even hesitate. "A relationship, commitment, everything."

Hope was throwing confetti in the air, clapping its hands and stomping its feet inside my chest. My heart felt yanked like a kite in a gust of wind, lifting it skyward. I clamped down hard, remembering that Gabriel wasn't even close to being ready for anything resembling a commitment. I had enough of my own issues with it. I couldn't be stupid all over again.

"Gabriel, you told me you would never commit to anyone. What's changed in a few months?" I knew, I freaking *knew* I shouldn't be asking these questions, but I couldn't seem to help myself.

"I figured something out."

I forgot to breathe and was suddenly gulping in air. Gathering myself together after several breaths, with the brisk wind giving me an assist as it swirled into the space, I asked, "What's that?"

"I love you," he stated as though it was no big deal.

For the third time today, tears stung my eyes. This time I couldn't hold back and leaned my head down, pressing the heels of my hands into my eye sockets. I would *not* fall apart in front of him.

After a moment, the muddle of emotion inside lasered in on anger. It gave me the impetus to lift my eyes again. I didn't even care if he could tell I was trying not to cry. "What the fuck, Gabriel? This is bullshit. Do not fuck with my emotions like this."

Chapter Four

GABRIEL

Okay, so this wasn't going well. Nora was really upset.

I forged ahead anyway. "I'm not fucking with you or your emotions. I'm trying to be honest."

She snatched up her bowl of macaroni and cheese and stuffed a bite in her mouth, chewing fiercely. After she swallowed, she said, "I can't have this conversation. Not now."

"Can you listen?"

She stuffed another bite of macaroni into her mouth, chewing as if her life depended on it. After a moment, she nodded jerkily.

Because the rapid pace of my heartbeat was wearing me out, I thought maybe she had the right idea. I took a few bites of my own food to try to calm down. The wind blew wild, and a sense of relief settled over me. Maybe I *had* totally screwed this up, like epically, but I could get us through to the other side of this. It might take some time, but it was worth the wait.

The crazy part was the relief I felt at having Nora furious at me. It was so much better than the cold, gray wall of silence she'd created between us. It had taken that for me to realize just how much she meant to me.

She'd indicated she would listen, so I needed to figure out what the hell I wanted to say. After several moments of nothing but the sound of the wind howling while we ate, I said, "I didn't think I wanted commitment, but I do. With you."

Nora had finished her food and was wiping the bowl out with a paper towel. Her eyes swung to mine. She regarded me quietly for several echoing beats of my heart.

"I don't know, Gabriel," she finally said. "We both have plenty of baggage."

"What do you mean?" I pressed.

"I have a father who never bothered to stick around. He also couldn't be bothered to be a father, and he was a shitty partner to my mother. You have a mom who was hardly there. We're not a great pair. Let's just try to be friends."

"Friends?"

Oh, now *I* was getting angry. For fuck's sake, I did not want to be polite and friendly with her. I wanted to *be* with her.

She stood, holding a hand out and wiggling her fingers in my direction. "What?" I asked.

"Give me your bowl. I'll go rinse it off in the ocean with mine."

"I'll go with you," I said, just to be contrary.

She rolled her eyes and turned away. I carefully slid over the piece of plywood I'd placed outside the shed and moved the bag of gravel holding it in place. As I leaned both against the side of the structure, I was positive the plywood was there for the very reason we'd used it.

Alaska was a funny place to live. If you lived here for more than a full round of seasons, you learned right quick that you needed to be prepared at all times. No doubt others had got stuck here at some point due to the weather.

The wind was still howling, and I watched as it blew Nora's brown curls in a swirl around her head. We stopped at the water's edge. Even though it was late summer, the water was freezing cold. Beaches in Alaska didn't draw many sunbathers or even swimmers. Most people who had the nerve to go in the water wore a wetsuit. Those who didn't usually wished they had.

After we rinsed off our bowls and spoons, we walked together back to the planes. Nora had everything put away in a few minutes. Looking up at the sky, she stuffed her hands in her pockets as she leaned against the side of her plane.

"We should sleep in my plane together."

Her eyes whipped to mine. She opened her mouth to reply before snapping it shut, pressing her lips in a line. As much as I wanted a night with Nora in my arms again, that wasn't why I suggested that. Evenings were seriously chilly here, no matter what time of year. The temperature could easily drop into the forties and probably would. Not to mention, I'd already taken a gander in the back of her plane, and it was stacked with mail that couldn't be delivered until I got back over here to patch up that wing.

"Fine," she muttered.

We passed the time playing cards until the sun finally slipped below the horizon. Nora didn't pretend I was invisible, but warm wasn't how I would describe her.

We went to sleep in the back of the plane after I

moved two of the passenger seats. Nora's back was to me with her sleeping bag zipped up tight. With the wind dancing in a push and pull between the land and the ocean, I fell asleep to the rhythmic gusts and wondered how I could fix the fracture I'd created between us. Because with Nora, when it was good, it was so, *so* good.

Chapter Five

NORA

Feeling toasty warm, I burrowed closer to Gabriel's always comforting and solid form. He had an arm curled around my shoulders, and I was shamelessly plastered against his chest. Despite the cold metal under my sleeping bag and the howling wind, I'd slept better last night than I had in months.

Until my brain flickered online, and I remembered I wasn't supposed to be with Gabriel. *Fuck.* I didn't realize my inside thought had formed into an audible whisper until he replied.

"Well, if that's how you want to start the day, I'm down for that." The low rumble of his teasing tone vibrated through me.

Without any way to finesse this moment, I propped myself up on an elbow. His eyes were open. He stared at me with a sleepy, sensual look I knew well.

Longing pierced me so sharply it almost hurt. I glanced around us, surveying the situation. There wasn't much room back here.

Somehow, my sleeping bag was no longer zipped.

As much as I wanted to blame it on Gabriel, I knew better. That didn't stop me from trying. When my eyes made their way back to his, I said, "You unzipped my sleeping bag."

"Nice try, but no." He shook his head. His hand was splayed low on my waist, just above my bottom. My knee was tucked over his muscled thigh. I supposed I should be grateful I hadn't stripped myself naked in my apparently crazed desire to get close to him.

"It's quiet outside," I observed.

"Wind's down. We can leave."

He hadn't moved. Because of the placement of my knee, I was acutely aware of his arousal. And mine. I could feel the slick heat of it between my thighs. This was what happened when I ended up alone with Gabriel. Every ounce of my sensibility flew out the window.

I wanted to kiss him so badly, my lips were tingling.

The distinct sound of a small plane engine in the distance was enough to snap me out of this insane reverie. I scrambled away from him. In a matter of minutes, we were both out of the plane. I walked to the edge of the shoreline and splashed icy-cold ocean water on my face. It was bracing, but it sure as hell woke me up.

After I'd given him the go-ahead to use my little camp stove, he'd started boiling some water. When I returned to the plane, he gestured toward a small coffee filter propped over a container. "Coffee is brewing. Keep an eye on it. I'll be right back."

A plane flew over us as Gabriel waved and strode to the water, doing the same as I had, splashing his face and drying it with a towel. We both had travel toothbrushes and the like. I was impatient for the coffee and watched as it drained slowly through the filter.

By the time we were getting ready to fly, I was relieved to have some caffeine in my system. Gabriel was running through the pre-flight checks when he said, "I meant it. I love you."

Tears pricked my eyes, and my throat felt thick. For me, trying to find trust in someone else was akin to trying to catch leaves blowing in the wind. I didn't want him to see me crying, so I looked away. I watched the stunning view through a blur as the plane lifted into the sky while the familiar sound of the engine rumbled.

When he reached across and curled his hand over where mine rested on top of my thigh, I told myself to swat his touch away. Yet I couldn't make myself do it.

———

The paneled ceiling above my head had exactly sixteen knots in the wood. Bored with counting them, I rolled to my side and stared out the window.

With the help of my two brothers and the other guys who worked at the resort, I'd built this small house myself. I'd specifically wanted a window level with my bed so I could see the moon and the stars at night. I'd never been a great sleeper, so I wanted a view when I woke. Too many nights as a little girl of being startled awake when my father came home, usually drunk, had made sleep elusive for me. My parents would argue, and it would sound sharp and broken, leaving my nerves jangling as I lay alone in bed.

I always felt a pinch of relief when he would

disappear again. Tangled within that relief, I struggled with the unsettled weight of my mother's worry about money. In short, I hadn't slept well since childhood.

When I woke up, I wanted a nice view at night because even though my father had passed away years ago, I still slept restlessly. I supposed the habits formed in childhood were hard to break, especially when it came to sleep and the way the unconscious held sway.

There were no moon and stars to look at this morning. The sun was marching up the sky, dew glistening on the fireweed spread out in front of me. The pretty weed stood tall with its bright fuchsia petals, filling many a field in Alaska's landscape. If it wasn't so abundant, it would be worth cultivating. These fields of fuchsia started in late summer and rolled through fall until the petals fell and coated the ground with their bright whimsy until they faded.

Even Alaska's stunning views couldn't soothe the restlessness in my heart and mind this morning. I kicked back the covers and snagged my phone from my bedside table. Even though it was a tiny bit cowardly, I elected to call Daphne instead of anyone else at the lodge.

"Morning!" She greeted me with more cheer than I was prepared for.

"Good morning," I replied. "I'm not feeling well. Could you let Flynn know? I don't have any official flights scheduled because we canceled them all yesterday."

"Are you okay? Can I get you anything?" Daphne pressed, her honest concern twisting my heart a little.

"I'll be okay. I feel a migraine coming on. I'll knock back some ibuprofen, and I should feel better in a little while." I was lying, but I didn't feel like dealing with anyone this morning.

"Okay. Call over here if you need anything."

I hung up and stared at my feet dangling off the edge of my tall four-poster bed. My toenails were painted bright blue. My seventeen-year-old sister, Cat, had wanted to paint them the other evening. I laughed a little at my toes before shimmying off the bed.

While I didn't have a migraine, I did have a mild headache. More than that, though, I didn't know what to do and wasn't up for facing the tight group of friends and family I lived and worked with. I believed that Gabriel believed what he said about loving me. I just knew all too well how much my baggage couldn't tolerate the fracture in our relationship after he'd so bluntly told me he couldn't consider commitment months ago.

It had all started stupidly. Friends with benefits seemed easy enough to do. Because I believed I would never fall for anyone. I thought I was too smart for that. Gabriel and I had serious chemistry, the kind that burned like a hot flare in the sky. I figured it might be complicated because he was one of my brother's best friends, but I thought I could manage it. I also thought that flare would eventually burn out, but it didn't. Apparently, our chemistry was of the peat fire variety. It felt destined to burn into infinity.

I turned these thoughts over in my mind while the hot water ran down over me in the shower. I wished I hadn't gone and fallen in love with Gabriel. Stupid, stupid, stupid.

Even though I thought it was impossible for me to trust, I wanted to. When what was supposed to be a fun fling with a friend turned into much more in my heart, I wasn't thinking clearly. I felt safe with Gabriel and told him I wanted more than our sort of secret friends-with-benefits arrangement. But he'd slapped down that idea hard and fast.

By the time I was dressed in my comfortable lounge around the house clothes, a fuzzy fleece top and buttery soft leggings, I was ready to spend the day watching distracting television. I was on my way to getting over Gabriel even if he thought he loved me.

Halfway through a cup of coffee and an episode of a baking show, I heard a knock on my door. I stared over at the door curiously. Aside from my family and anyone else who worked at the resort, people didn't just drop by, not out here.

I stood, crossing to the door cautiously. When I peered out the side window and saw it was Daphne, relief coursed through me. I swung the door open.

"Hey," I said, wondering why she was here.

Daphne's green eyes twinkled. "Hey, I brought you some soup." She held up a plastic container. "It's still warm." She also had a cloth bag looped over her arm.

Opening the door wider, I gestured her through. "You're too good to me."

"Your place is so freaking cute," she said as she walked past me.

Her auburn hair was pulled up in a braid that was spun in a circle and pinned in place. Daphne was petite, curvy, and incredible, giving off this highly competent and tidy vibe. My brother had fallen for her so hard it was a joke among the rest of us. We all adored her, though, and she was the best thing ever for him. She guarded his heart like the fierce woman she was.

"What kind of soup is it?" I asked as I followed her over to the table in the kitchen area.

My downstairs had an open living room and

kitchen with a woodstove situated against the back wall, which was practically standard-issue in Alaska. Wide-plank hardwood flooring throughout the house gave the space a warm feel. The living room area took up most of the downstairs with a loveseat and two chairs facing the television mounted on the wall. Windows to the other side offered a view of a field with trees scattered through it.

An oval table served as a divider between the kitchen and living area. Beside the back entrance was a laundry room and bathroom. A spiral staircase in the corner of the living room led up to a landing with a master bedroom with its own bathroom and a spare bedroom. I'd made sure to install a nice soaking tub along with an excellent shower.

"It's chicken and dumpling soup," Daphne said as she stopped by the kitchen counter. "You can have that for lunch. I also brought you fresh bagels with smoked salmon cream cheese. Perfect for a migraine."

The moment I met her gaze, I knew she knew I'd been lying about having a migraine.

"I don't have a migraine," I said with a sheepish smile. "I did have a headache, though. I wasn't lying about that."

After setting the container and the bag on the counter, she pulled out the bagels wrapped in foil. She also produced two distinct red coffee cups. "Oh my God, is that Cammi's coffee?"

She smiled. "Of course. Elias brought some over for us. This cup has your name on it."

Cammi owned Red Truck Coffee and Misty Mountain Café, the two best coffee shops in Diamond Creek. We were blessed with frequent personal deliveries from her boyfriend and our good friend, who used to live out here at the resort and still worked with us. Cammi had stolen his heart, and we got the plus of getting her coffee on the regular.

"Bonus," I said, holding my hand out for the cup. "I made my own cup, but it's not as good."

Daphne shrugged. "My coffee can't compete with hers either. I even tried to have her teach me. I'm convinced she adds a secret ingredient."

I chuckled as we sat down at the table. "One for yourself?" I asked when I saw her carrying two bagels wrapped in foil.

"Of course. We're having breakfast together."

We sat down and enjoyed some coffee, bagels, and quiet. One of my favorite things about Daphne was she never felt the need to fill the silence. She was easy to be with.

Besides the fact that I was totally a fan of her relationship with my brother, we had scored one of the best chefs I'd ever known in my entire life for the resort due to their relationship.

I looked over at her after my third bite of bagel. "Speaking of secrets, maybe that's why you're such a good baker. You put something magic in these."

The bagel was the perfect texture of chewy and light. I had no idea how she pulled it off. The cream cheese had just enough flavor not to be overwhelming. Smoked salmon required a balance because it could easily tip into an overpowering flavor.

She laughed softly. "No special secrets. I love food, and I don't mind trying things again and again until I get it just right. I feel like my cooking skills have improved since I've been here because I have plenty of testers. Y'all are the best taste testers ever," she said in her soft Southern twang.

"You know me, I will taste test all day. I don't know

how useful I am, though. I think my palate is biased in favor of everything you make."

Daphne laughed again. With her lightly freckled cheeks and bow-shaped mouth, she was so pretty.

"I'm assuming there were no hitches in the flight schedule. Someone would've called me by now if there were."

She pursed her lips, cocking her head to the side. "I think you forgot someone needed to go with Gabriel to deal with your plane today. I told Flynn to leave you alone. He got Trey Holden to help out with some flights. Trey was thrilled because he hasn't been able to fly in a few months."

"Oh, sorry. I totally spaced that."

She shrugged slightly. "No problem. They worked it out. Trey took over Diego's flights, and Diego went with Gabriel. Flynn says Gabriel's the best mechanic in the bunch anyway."

"He only had to replace that landing tire and patch that area on the wing," I muttered, feeling sheepish. No matter how frustrated I felt toward Gabriel, I didn't like to create extra work for anyone, even if it was unintentional.

Daphne nodded, finishing a bite of her bagel. "What's up with you and Gabriel?"

My cheeks felt hot instantly. But I managed a breath and gathered my composure. "Nothing, why do you ask?"

"Oh, for God's sake, stop lying," she retorted pertly.

"What do you mean?" I ground out.

"This isn't the first time we've talked about you and Gabriel."

I took a bite of my bagel, chewing good and hard. Maybe I could chew my feelings away. Daphne was annoying me now. She patiently waited, perfectly comfortable with the silence and my delayed response.

After I finished chewing, I set my bagel down, rested my elbows on the table, and leaned my face into my hands. On the heels of a deep breath, I gathered the courage to meet her eyes again and lifted my head, letting my hands fall to the table. "Nothing is going on with us. He told me he never wanted to get serious months ago."

Daphne circled her hand in the air, looking bored. "Right. I knew that. You've been working the cold routine on him mighty hard. But something happened yesterday. You faked having a migraine this morning, and you never call out of work. Meanwhile, Gabriel looks like a lost puppy."

My heart gave an achy thump, and tears stung my eyes. I hated how emotional he made me feel. I knew no one else could *make* me feel anything, but whatever.

"He wasn't supposed to pick you up yesterday. Did he tell you that?" she asked softly.

"I thought he and Elias switched up the schedule. What do you mean?" My heartbeat was galloping in my chest while confusion and sadness and the usual storm of emotions that Gabriel stirred up swirled through me.

"It was going to be Elias, but Gabriel asked him to switch when Elias mentioned you needed to hitch a flight with someone. Elias was happy to do it because it meant he got home earlier. Gabriel called Flynn after that."

All I could do was stare at her. "He made it sound like Elias asked to change the schedule. That's crazy," I said slowly.

"Is it? Elias said Gabriel was all freaked out when he happened to mention he was changing his route for the afternoon. What happened with Gabriel? And don't you dare tell me nothing. I saw him this morning and now you."

"He told me he loves me, and us not being together made him realize how he felt." My words came out in a rush.

Daphne's impatience was showing when she circled a hand in the air again, her eyes widening. "That's it?"

I pursed my lips and cast her a glare. "That's all that happened. Well, then I had to sleep with him in the back of the plane because of the stupid wind. Oh, and he kissed me," I mumbled.

"Isn't this what you wanted?"

"Before, but not now. I had time to think too. Gabriel and I have opposite baggage. He's got commitment and trust issues because of his mother, and I have them because of my father. It's a bad combination."

My friend narrowed her eyes. "I think you're being ridiculous and looking for excuses."

"I only talked to you about him before because you promised you would keep your mouth shut. Don't start on me." I was feeling defensive and maybe overreacting, but I was trying to keep my shit together over Gabriel.

"I promised I wouldn't gossip," she insisted, her eyes flashing. "I didn't promise not to call you on it when you're doing the equivalent of cutting off your own nose to spite your face."

I felt like I was being scolded by a schoolteacher as she looked at me across the table. To add to the image, she lifted her napkin and dabbed at the corners of her mouth.

I sighed. "I know, I know. I need time to think. We

already had our own baggage that had nothing to do with each other, and then he went and made some more for me. He was crystal clear he never wanted to get serious with anyone, and now, all of a sudden, he does. With me?" I snorted at that. "What does Flynn know?"

"I don't know what he knows today. He knew you guys were fooling around before. He thought it was ridiculous, but he let you think it was a secret because he knows how private you are. I think he might've given Gabriel a little hell when you cut things off, but that's all I know. As far as whether or not Gabriel's talked to him today, I doubt it. There wasn't time. Flynn had an early transport run, so he was gone before we even had breakfast," she explained.

I shook my head. "I don't know why Gabriel suddenly thinks he's in love with me."

"Because he's had time to think. Sometimes we have to screw up before we realize what matters. That's not exactly a problem specific to him."

I swallowed through the thickness in my throat and rubbed my knuckles over my breastbone as if I could somehow smooth away the pain in my heart. It didn't make a bit of difference.

"Maybe you could try to talk to him again," Daphne said, her tone gentle.

"Are you going to nag me about this?" I jammed another bite of bagel in my mouth, annoyed she was ruining such a good breakfast.

"No. I mean, maybe. I care about you. I hate to see you throw a good thing away just because you're angry."

"I'm not angry," I lied.

She pursed her lips, her eyes taking on a knowing glint as she looked at me across the table.

"Okay, maybe I'm still a little angry," I fessed up.

"Ya think? Honey, you've managed not to speak to the guy for months. It's remarkable, really. It's been impressive."

I couldn't help the laugh that slipped out. "Fine. I was going to anyway, even without the lecture."

"Was that really a lecture?" Her tone was warm as she looked over at me.

"No, it wasn't. Thanks for being a friend." I offered a sheepish smile.

"Come up to the kitchen with me? I'd like some company, and all the guys are gone. Nobody's gonna be back before tonight, so you're in the clear. We can have a girls' day."

Chapter Six

NORA

Daphne and I ended up having a nice day, considering my unsettled mood from the morning. She let the topic of Gabriel go, and we finished watching a few episodes of a baking show together before we headed over to the resort kitchen.

My small house was a stone's throw through the trees to the lodge. Whenever I was crossing the gravel parking area and looked ahead to the resort, a sense of pride rolled through me. Flynn had returned home to Alaska to finish this half-built resort when he left the Air Force to take care of my younger sister and me. I was sixteen at the time and deep into being a moody teenager.

Our brother Grant had just started college when our mother died. Our father had passed away a few years before her, and Flynn's father had never been around. Our mother's track record with men held strong. She had children with two different men who didn't want much of anything to do with her or their kids. While Flynn's father had never been around, ours had bounced in and out of our lives like a ping pong ball.

As soon as Flynn landed in Alaska, he dived into a whirlwind of work. He'd turned what my mother and father had begun in fits and starts into a busy expedition resort. The three-story octagonal structure was a modern timber-frame building. The main floor had ample open space with several areas for guests.

Through an archway off the main area was the large kitchen with a view of the mountains and the ocean bay in the distance. The kitchen was open to guests as well. Daphne worked her magic there, cooking meals for the staff and up to thirty guests on any given day. All the guest rooms occupied the upper floors, and Flynn and Daphne, along with my youngest sister, Cat, stayed in a private apartment on the main floor.

For the past few summers, we'd spent time constructing a house where the rest of the staff stayed except me. As the only girl, I'd wanted my own space, and the house felt too much like living in a giant bachelor pad.

After Daphne and I returned to the resort, we got to work. I was a not-so-great cook, but I was an excellent assistant. Daphne worked her magic while I chopped vegetables and basically did whatever she said. Once we finished later that afternoon, we sat relaxing at the long table situated in front of the windows in the dining area.

I snagged one of the fresh sweet potato fries Daphne had made, letting out a moan as the flavor of lightly seasoned chipotle fries crossed my tongue. "Oh, my God, these are good. Why can't I cook like you?"

My question was rhetorical, but I knew the answer. Sometimes just getting food on the table was a miracle, given how little money my mother had at times when we were growing up. I was an expert at heating up soup in cans and making meals out of boxes. That was the extent of my cooking repertoire.

"I keep telling you I'll teach you," Daphne offered.

"I know, but I feel so ridiculous. I should know how to cook by now."

"It doesn't matter when you learn. Not everybody loves to cook, but it's nice to be able to handle the basics yourself."

At that moment, the door from the back hallway swung open, and Cat came through.

"Hey," she said, lifting her hand in a wave as she walked immediately into the pantry, returning with a box of crackers.

"We have sweet potato fries," Daphne called over when Cat stopped by the sink to fill a glass with water.

"Oh, good," Cat replied. "Those are better than crackers." She returned the crackers to the pantry before joining us at the table.

"What's up?" I asked.

My little sister was seventeen years old now, and I still couldn't quite believe it. Cat and my two brothers shared my mother's dark blond hair and slate-blue eyes, while I'd inherited my father's coloring. Cat's hair was pulled back in a lopsided ponytail. A quick glance at her puffy eyes and flushed cheeks, and I guessed she'd been crying. The corners of her lips were pinched tight and her shoulders hunched as she leaned back in her chair and folded a foot under her knee.

"I just got home from school," she replied.

"Thanks for the detail. I wouldn't have guessed," I replied dryly.

When Cat didn't smile, I knew for sure she was upset. "You okay?" I asked gently.

She took a shuddery breath. "No." Her glum tone matched her downcast eyes as she stretched her arm across the table to grab a few sweet potato fries.

"What happened?" Daphne asked.

"I broke up with Tanner."

"Oh, sweetie, what happened?" I scooted my chair closer to hers and slipped my arm across her back, rubbing my palm in a light circle between her shoulder blades.

"He cheated on me. I really liked him too," Cat said morosely.

"He did not!" Daphne said fiercely, her eyes practically blazing.

"Well, he's an idiot," I added.

"That's what I told him," Cat muttered.

"How did you find out?" Daphne asked.

Cat took a swallow of her water and fetched two more sweet potato fries, chewing one before she replied. "Shannon told me. She saw a text message he sent the other girl. I don't even like that girl, and I'm glad she's not my friend. I don't need someone like him either."

"Obviously, she's not your friend. You're a good friend," I said.

My sister cast me a swift little smile. "I know. I'm upset, but I'll be fine. I am worth more than having someone treat me like that." She lifted her chin.

"Absolutely," I commented.

Cat's eyes slid to mine. "I'm fine, you know. I was sad and angry, and I cried, but I'm fine."

"We know you'll be fine," Daphne interjected. "But we want to be there for you. Should we go kick his ass?"

Cat giggled. "You two could totally kick his ass. Oh my God, he would freak out."

"Flynn's going to ask about him. I was supposed to take him on that day fishing trip next weekend." Cat sighed heavily. "Will you make sure Flynn doesn't tell the rest of the guys?" Her eyes bounced between Daphne and me.

"Of course. It's your privacy. You don't even have to tell Flynn everything," I suggested. "You can just say you broke up if that's all you want to mention."

Cat rolled her eyes. "One of you will end up telling him by accident, so I'd rather it be me. It's not that I don't trust you. It's just, well, you're in love with him." She gave Daphne a pointed look before her eyes swung to me. "And sometimes you just let things slip when you're not thinking."

I gave her a sheepish smile. "I know. Downside of being an older sister. I only let them slip with Flynn, though."

Cat grinned. "I think Tanner was surprised, and I told him off right in the cafeteria. I don't care if I embarrassed him. I always promised myself I was never gonna be like our mom. She was literally a freaking doormat for our dad. Fuck that."

Daphne and I opened our mouths simultaneously before our gazes collided. I thought Daphne had been about to correct Cat's use of language, just like me. I shrugged. Sometimes the occasion called for it.

"Can I have some wine?" Cat asked next.

"No!" Daphne and I exclaimed in unison.

Cat burst out laughing. "I thought I'd try. When you dump a guy, it's good to have a drink and feel better, or something like that."

My hand slid off her back as I chuckled. "Sure, a glass of wine can help you relax here and there, but it's definitely not necessary. I'd rather have a friend be there for me than that."

Cat rolled her eyes. "Sure. Says you, who pours extra wine whenever Gabriel spends too much time around you."

Daphne bit her bottom lip, standing quickly and striding into the kitchen. Her shoulders were shaking, and I knew she was laughing. Of course, my very perceptive younger sister would've noticed a detail like that.

I decided it wasn't worth engaging in *that* dialogue and snagged another fry to pop into my mouth.

"I'm going to start teaching Nora how to cook. Want to help?" Daphne called over.

Cat brightened and straightened in her chair. "Yes. You can't have my job, though."

I laughed softly. "Sweetie, I don't think I'll ever get good enough at cooking to steal your kitchen job. I'm thrilled Flynn officially has you on the payroll."

Cat stood and skipped over toward the kitchen counter when Daphne began pulling things out to finish prepping for dinner. Guests would be returning from wherever they'd spent their day over the next few hours, and she would have dinner ready. Meanwhile, I needed to decide if I wanted to deal with seeing Gabriel tonight. I was leaning toward *not* when Cat called, "Come help me now. I'm going to prep a few game hens for roasting."

I was swept into being Cat's assistant for the next hour or so. When Gabriel arrived, I purposely didn't pour extra wine for myself. I could handle him, or so I told myself again and again. And again.

It didn't help that I felt the heat of his gaze on me. It *definitely* didn't help when he slipped onto a stool beside me at the counter surrounding the area where Daphne was working.

"Your plane's good to go," he said, his low, gravelly voice sending shivers chasing over my skin.

When I risked a glance at him and ran right into the intense beam of his gaze, butterflies took flight, spinning wildly in my belly while I tried to catch my breath.

I was *so* screwed.

GABRIEL

"What?" Diego asked.

He leaned against the plane, crossing his arms over his bulky chest and lasering me with his way-too-perceptive gaze.

"I told her I loved her," I said, practically itching all over with the discomfort at saying *that* word out loud. It had come easy when I said it to Nora, but it made me feel a little crazy with anyone else. All of my friends knew I'd never planned to get serious with anyone.

Diego pinched the bridge of his nose as his head dipped down, and he let out a sigh. "And then what?" His eyes lifted to mine again.

I closed the small storage compartment underneath the plane and turned the latch to lock it before straightening. "I told her I wanted us to try again, or something like that," I mumbled.

Diego regarded me with that quiet intensity he always carried. "Dude, I love you like a brother, but that was stupid."

"How was that stupid? I was telling her how I felt." Defensiveness flared inside.

"It's not a magic word. The last time you two had a serious conversation about the state of your relationship, you told her you could never be serious with anyone, especially not her because she's Flynn's sister," my friend pointed out. "So you open with, 'I love you,' and assume that's just gonna solve it all." He snapped his fingers in the air for emphasis.

"Dude, I don't know how to do this. I've never been serious with anyone. Just tell me what to do, and I'll do it. Because that definitely didn't work," I said flatly.

Diego chuckled, running a hand through his rumpled dark hair. "I don't have all the answers."

"Yeah, but you've been in a serious relationship more than once. You and Gemma are doing great, and you were engaged before." I held up two fingers. "That's *way* more experience than me."

He leaned his head against the plane and groaned. "I was too young to understand love when I was engaged before, and Gemma and I are pretty fresh. That said, I'm not afraid of commitment, not the way you are. My parents had a rock-solid marriage, so I had something to learn from. I think maybe take it a little slower with Nora. I do think it's good you told her how you felt."

I must've looked as flummoxed as I felt because he pressed on. "She needs to know how you feel, but after what you told her before, you can't assume she'll believe it's that easy. She was pretty hurt. It's been months since she actually spoke to you. I guess you can take it as a win that she replied with words." He cast me a wry smile at that.

I took a few strides, sitting down on an overturned

crate and resting my elbows on my knees. I stared at the floor, my eyes landing on an oil stain. Repairing my relationship with Nora, if I could even pull it off, was *way* harder than getting that oil stain out of the floor, and that was basically impossible with concrete.

"I'm glad you figured out how you felt," Diego offered, his tone encouraging.

Lifting my head, I shrugged. "It's not really gonna matter if she won't give us a chance."

Diego arched a brow. "Let's go grab some pizza. Elias texted me and was wondering if we could meet him. Maybe he can give you some advice."

"Jesus, just what I need. Advice about my love life."

"Not about your love life, your *lack* of a love life," Diego teased, clapping my shoulder lightly as I stood from the crate.

We locked up the plane hangar and headed over to Glacier Pizza.

A short while later, I leaned back in the booth, letting out a satisfied sigh. "Man, they have the best pizza."

Elias grinned from across the table as he finished off the last slice from the large pizza we'd gotten for the three of us. "Damn straight."

Diego returned from the restroom, slipping into the booth beside me. "What did I miss?"

"Absolutely nothing," I offered with a chuckle.

"I have some news, actually," Elias commented.

"Lay it on us." Diego leaned his elbows on the table.

"Cammi's pregnant." Elias's brown eyes lit up when he smiled, shaking his head in wonderment.

Diego thumped his fist over his heart as he leaned back. "Congratulations. I know y'all wanted this."

I dipped my head, leaning over across the table to

clasp my friend's shoulder and squeeze it lightly. "Congratulations. How are you feeling about it?"

"I can't fucking believe it. I'm equal parts terrified and excited."

"How far along is she?" Diego asked.

"Three months. Apparently, that's the magic number when you're allowed to start telling people," Elias offered with a grin. "Also, we're getting married soon."

"Wow," I said, shaking my head slightly. "You've gone from committed to being single to about to be a father. I can't believe it."

Diego grinned. "I can believe it. He found the right woman."

"Does that mean you and Gemma are thinking kids already?" I teased.

Diego shrugged. "When the time is right, I'm ready. I love kids."

Our waiter stopped by the table, effectively interrupting the conversation. I was relieved to have a moment to gather myself. I was kind of stunned by how easily Elias had accepted the shift in his life.

Elias and I had been tight for years, just as all of us working at Walker Adventures were. Yet Elias and I shared a common grievance. Both of us had been betrayed by another friend, Greg. Greg had died, but he'd been a core part of our group in the Air Force. That group had parlayed me into this job when Flynn called me about it. I loved being here and crisscrossing the skies in Alaska. Greg had screwed around with Elias's girlfriend and even gotten her pregnant before he died. Before that, he'd also screwed around with a girl I'd been seeing. Maybe I hadn't been serious, but it still wasn't cool. Not even a little.

She had even approached me a few times after the

fact with apologies, wishing we could try again. Fat fucking chance of that. I had enough issues with commitment. I didn't need to try it with someone I couldn't trust.

After we left the pizza place, I ended up driving Elias back to the place he now shared with Cammi. Apparently, he needed some new tires, and he'd dropped his truck off. We were in silence for most of the short drive, but just as I was turning down the road that led to their house, Elias said, "You know, it feels good to move on."

I slid my gaze sideways, but he was looking forward. "What do you mean?"

"Cynicism is cold comfort in the long run," he offered cryptically. "How are things with you and Nora?"

I let out a sigh. "Not great. She finally spoke to me for the first time in months when I went to pick her up the other day."

Elias chuckled. "Ah. So it was worth asking me to rearrange my whole schedule."

I laughed, although I felt a little hollow, and my heart ached. "I suppose. I need to do more than get her talking."

"If she didn't care, she wouldn't be angry," he replied.

I pondered that as I drove out to the resort in the darkness. The stars appeared close enough for me to reach up and grab them, and the moonlight glittered on the water.

———

The following morning, my phone rang just as I was walking into my bedroom from the shower. I yanked on a pair of sweatpants and rubbed a towel over my chest as I crossed over to glance down at my phone where it sat on my dresser.

I was going to ignore the call, but then it began ringing again. Lifting it, I slid my thumb across the screen. "Hey, Mom."

"Gabriel!" she exclaimed, sounding surprised that I answered. As if she hadn't just dialed my number twice in a row.

"What's up?" I asked.

"Tell me how you're doing," my mom said brightly.

"I'm fine, Mom. How are you?"

I looped the towel around the bedpost and crossed over to stare out the window.

"I'm okay," she said slowly before pausing.

I sensed she didn't know what else to say. My mom and I weren't close. The only way to describe what she'd done when I was a kid was abandonment. She left our dad to take care of us and bounced in and out of our lives periodically when she needed something.

I used to resent her, but I realized it was eating me up, so I'd made peace with my resignation for what she was to me. She usually called when she needed money, and I usually gave it to her.

I waited. I wasn't going to fill the silence for her.

"I'm looking into buying a house," she finally said, "but I could use a little more rent money until then."

"How much do you need?"

I ignored the disappointment that settled like a thin, worn blanket over my shoulders. I was resigned to this, but it didn't mean I liked it.

"Well, my rent's a thousand bucks a month. I hope you don't think I called you just for money."

I rolled my eyes, marveling at how well-defended she was. My mother's denial was a force of its own.

She could ask me for money every time she called and still try to insist that wasn't why she called. I focused on the view outside my windows. The sun was rising, casting a shimmery golden glow over the dark mountains and jagged peaks. We already had termination dust, the first fresh snow that fell on the mountains. I wondered when it would snow at our elevation.

"It's no problem, Mom," I replied. "Same account?"

"Yes."

She paused, and I could practically imagine her wherever she was sitting. Her legs were usually crossed with one foot bouncing restlessly. Her fingers were either holding a cigarette as she smoked nervously or toying with whatever she could get her hands on.

"Have you heard from Aubrey?" she asked, her question falling like a sharp edge into the silence that spun out between us.

"We text every other week or so. She's gonna try to get up here one summer."

"Oh, okay." My mother's voice was hesitant, and I knew she didn't know what to say. My sister refused to talk to her.

"I'll make sure that money is wired over by tomorrow. I need to run because I have some flights scheduled for this morning."

"Okay. Talk to you soon. Thank you."

"You're welcome, Mom. Take care."

The line clicked in my ear when she hung up. I lowered my phone slowly, setting it on the windowsill. I rested my hands there and stared out. Dew was glittering on the dead grass and flowers. Autumn was passing quickly, and apparently, we had a wedding soon for Cammi and Elias.

I wondered if I could find what Elias had with Cammi. My mother was a big part of the reason I never thought I could commit. I'd told myself it wasn't worth it for years, so like an idiot, when Nora pressed and said she wanted more, I'd told her it wasn't possible.

I wanted to fix it, to take it back. I wanted to go back to us.

I thought about how Elias said he was equal parts excited and terrified to become a father. I wanted to have that kind of courage. Right now, all I wanted was to win her back, and I was terrified of losing the one woman I loved.

Chapter Eight

NORA

"Just freaking do what I say!"

After ordering the recalcitrant washer to obey me, I tried once more to shove it into place. It started to move. "Hallelujah!" I whisper-shouted to no one but myself and the washer that definitely could not care less about what I wanted it to do.

Just as I thought it was going my way, it shifted suddenly and slid way too fast. "Fuck!" Something pointy and painful jammed against my toe.

My eyes watered as I breathed through the sharp pain. It receded quickly, except now the washer was showing me who was boss. Somehow, I was pinned between it and the wall—or rather, my boot was— which meant I couldn't go anywhere.

I tried futilely to lift it with a few grunts and groans in the process. All the while, my toe throbbed painfully.

My gaze whisked around the small laundry room. I'd been so excited to finally save up enough money to buy a brand-new washer and dryer that I decided I could install them myself. Really, it shouldn't have been a big deal. I was a handy kind of girl. I'd hooked up the plumbing by myself, feeling ridiculously proud about it.

I didn't like to feel limited by my size, but in this case, clearly, the weight and bulk of this machine weren't working in my favor. With two older brothers, both tall, lanky, and plenty strong, I'd been *that* girl, the one who was always pushing to be stronger and faster than her brothers. To add kindling to that fire, I was a pilot who worked in Alaska. Most of my coworkers were men. It was a man's world in more ways than I preferred.

"Well," I said to myself—because I talked to myself a lot when I was working on things alone—"let's hope I can reach my phone."

I eyed my phone, sitting innocently on the windowsill. Leaning back, with the toe of my boot pinned firmly under the stupid washer, I grabbed it.

It almost slipped from my fingers, but I caught it on the descent. I dialed Daphne's cell phone first.

"Hey, you!"

I could hear the smile in her voice. "Hey, you got a minute?"

"I have a minute to talk, but in about five, I should reach town. Need anything from the grocery store? You never did reply to my text last night."

I groaned. "You're almost in town?"

"Yeah, I told you I was going to the grocery store and taking care of some other errands. What's up?"

"I'm kind of stuck," I said with a sigh.

"Stuck?"

"I sort of dropped the washer on my foot, and it's jammed."

"Come again?"

I let out another sigh, leaning my head back and

eyeing the ceiling. I'd painted that very ceiling myself. It was a perfectly smooth surface. No streaks, no ugly stains, absolutely nothing to focus on.

Lowering my gaze, I glanced between the wall and the washer. There wasn't much space, and I couldn't quite figure out why my foot was stuck.

"Who's here at the resort? Anyone?" I finally asked.

I mentally scanned the flight schedule since I handled all of the scheduling for our business. I almost groaned again when I realized the one and only pilot who was not in the air today, aside from me, was Gabriel.

"Gabriel should be at the staff house. He passed through the kitchen, trying to sweet-talk me into stealing some of the cookies I'm bringing to Cammi for her café," Daphne said with a laugh rustling in her throat. "I think you're going to have to call him. Cat's at school, so she won't be home for hours. Even if I hightail it back there, it's going to be at least twenty minutes. If you're desperate, though, I'll turn around."

I bit the insides of my cheeks to keep from begging. I didn't need to be so childish as to ask Daphne to drive all the way back to the resort and mess up her afternoon when I knew she needed to go to the store. It was dinner not only for the family but also for the guests. I couldn't impose on her like that.

"I'll call Gabriel," I grumbled.

"You sound like a sad child," Daphne teased. "You survived him flying you home last week. You can survive this."

"I know, I know. Since I forgot to text you last night, now I need some wine. Can you get my favorite, that sweet red that I like so much? On second thought, let's make margaritas. I'm gonna need a few tonight."

I could hear the amusement in Daphne's voice when she replied, "You got it, girl. Chin up. Let Gabriel save you again."

"Oh, shut up," I muttered.

She merely laughed before hanging up.

I glared at my phone for a moment. Like the washer, it had no reaction to me and my feelings.

I tapped open my screen and pulled up his contact. I had changed it to "Arrogant asshole" months ago when we broke things off. I didn't enjoy how my pulse raced as I tapped to call him, or the way my belly felt as if I were falling.

He answered on the first ring.

The seconds that stretched between me tapping to call him and the phone ringing felt like time was spinning out in slow motion. My heart was thumping wildly, and my belly shimmied with anxiety and anticipation. Much as I didn't want to ask for Gabriel's help, I wanted to see him, almost desperately. I missed him, I missed what we had, and I was beyond annoyed at him for trying to change the rules again.

"Nora?" his voice prompted, seemingly out of nowhere.

I'd lost the thread of my own thoughts.

"Hey, um, I need some help."

"Anything," he said so quickly that my heart twisted a little.

"I'm stuck. Just come over to my place. I need more strength than I have."

"Are you okay?" He sounded alarmed.

"Well, my toe hurts like hell, but I'll be fine. Just hurry, please."

"Be there in a few."

For the first time since I'd built my small house, I cursed that I'd wanted to make sure it was at least five minutes away from everybody else. My breath came out in an annoyed sigh.

I tried to shimmy the washer and finally realized why I was stuck. The flooring under the corner had been knocked loose, and my foot was caught between the edge of the tile and the wall. I'd left the gap there purposely to bring the plumbing up. Nobody ever saw behind the washer.

Fuck my life. This was a silly, minor mishap, but I felt foolish. Of course, it *had* to be Gabriel coming to help. Gabriel, who now claimed he loved me. Gabriel, who kissed me and set all those embers alight between us again. I'd just barely reached the point when I thought I could somehow get to the other side of falling for him. My anger had served me quite well, and I'd savored the cool blade of it for months.

Five minutes definitely hadn't passed when I heard him burst through the front door. "Nora!"

My heart twisted at the hint of fear in his voice.

"In the laundry room!"

A second later, he peered through the open doorway. His gaze chased over me. "You're stuck behind the washer?"

"Go ahead and laugh," I deadpanned. "I thought I could handle moving it myself."

He still looked concerned, and my heart twisted again. Everything felt so tricky with him. We'd finally spoken because I *had* to talk to him, and now I couldn't seem to climb back across that chasm I'd created between us and stay firmly on the opposite side where I could avoid him.

I felt as if I was walking a narrow rope bridge across the chasm, just wide enough that I could put one foot in front of the other. If I fell, I didn't know where I would land. My heart was already bruised and battered from when he told me he could never commit. *Never.* He'd actually used that word. I believed him.

Now, I spent every night since that stupid night I'd had to sleep beside him in the back of his plane, replaying our conversation and our kiss. I didn't know how to believe him now, and I couldn't get my own stupid heart to stop clamoring for me to give him a second chance.

My heart didn't have good judgment. My heart knew well the lessons I'd learned from my parents. Men weren't to be trusted. They were flaky and irresponsible, and you couldn't count on them. Ever.

Of course, ever since the first night Gabriel and I gave in to the flames flickering between us, he hadn't been with anybody else. That was why I'd been so foolish and thought maybe there was something to what I felt between us. Matters were made decisively more complicated by how insanely good it was with us. That man played my body like a fiddle, and the music was gorgeous. No one could make me forget myself as thoroughly as Gabriel could. I craved his touch.

"Nora?" he prompted.

See? That was how bad it was with him. I lost track of everything. I was just staring down at the silver washer. I lifted my eyes to his, bracing myself to take the hit that would come from looking into his gaze. Good thing I was prepared.

The jolt hit me hard when my gaze locked onto his mossy green eyes. My cells spun like tops, excited to see him. I felt as if the air around us contained sparks, sizzling in a fiery mist around us.

"I'm stuck," I repeated through the muddle of need clamoring in my body.

Gabriel glanced between the washer and the wall. "Your foot?"

"Yeah. I left a gap in the flooring for the plumbing, and my foot slid into it when I pulled this a little too hard. I can't get leverage to lift it."

Gabriel was gracious enough not to laugh at my predicament. His hands curled over the edges of the washer. In one smooth motion, he tilted it, and when the pressure eased off my foot, I couldn't hold back my sigh of relief.

Glancing at him, I asked, "Can you move it back a little now?"

Of course, he took care of it immediately with little effort. I shimmied out from the gap between the wall and the washer, and he put the washer back in place. He moved so quickly, I didn't even realize he was hooking it up as I shook my foot to relieve the pain from being cramped under the corner of the washer.

"Thank you," I said when he straightened.

"No problem. Your foot okay?"

"My toes will be sore, but I'll be fine," I said with a sheepish shrug.

Staying in the small room with him was dangerous. His presence filled it, potent and strong.

I practically ran out of the room, annoyed that I couldn't move that fast with my toe still throbbing. He followed me out. The laundry room was just off the kitchen. I rested my hips against the counter, and he stopped maybe a foot away. I wanted him to leave quickly, but that felt ungrateful, considering he'd run over here to help me.

"Have you thought about what I said?" His eyes

held mine, so earnest that my heart gave another tricky twist.

Butterflies amassed in my belly, and my breath got short as my pulse took off like a rocket into space. Being in actual space might create enough distance between Gabriel and me so I could get a hold of my anger again. That, and my sanity.

Unfortunately, my emotions were their own mess, and I felt tears hot in my eyes and had to close them. I was afraid I was going to cry right in front of him.

My fear was proven true when he said, "Please don't cry, Nora."

Oh, God. I felt him stepping closer and wrapping his strong arms around me. Just like I wanted. *So, so* much. I couldn't even bring myself to shove him away.

I tucked my head into the warm curve of his neck, and my traitorous arms slipped around his waist. I didn't burst into tears, although that was about the only thing I managed to keep under control. I breathed in his scent, a little crisp with a hint of ever-green clinging to him.

One of his hands cupped the back of my head, and the other slid up and down my back in what I thought he intended to be a soothing pass. I was so unsettled, so frantic that his touch stirred up desire, and sparks flew, catching fire inside me. I willed my pulse to slow, tried to scramble for some kind of control, but my control slipped, and I savored the feel of him.

It was quiet, save for the resounding beat of my heart. It drummed out recklessly, overjoyed at being close to Gabriel once again. I couldn't seem to get my heart to recognize the risk. I was certain Gabriel only thought he loved me because I'd put a stop to our convenient relationship.

I didn't doubt he *wanted* me. I knew chemistry

when I felt it, and ours was of the barn burner variety. With my heart and my body staking their claim on this moment, my anxious mind was reduced to a distant murmur.

A profound sense of relief also filtered through me. I was tired of listening to my own worries, playing on a loop of regret and recrimination. I didn't have my own heartbreak before Gabriel, not romantically speaking. I simply had my entire childhood shaping my understanding of what it meant to love someone who didn't share the same concepts of commitment and loyalty.

For now, though, that noise faded into the background. I could hear Gabriel's heartbeat beneath my ear. He was warm and strong, and I was tired. My mind scrambled as if it had slipped and fallen and was trying to catch its balance again, but it was unsteady. I told myself I would just let him hold me. That was it. Nothing more.

His fingers started to sift through my hair, and I practically purred like a cat, nuzzling a little closer. My nose had landed just over the open vee of his Henley shirt. His skin was warm, and his scent overtook my senses. Before I knew it, I was the foolish one. My thoughts slipped again, left behind in the cacophony of a roaring desire and sheer emotional overwhelm.

My lips landed in that triangle of skin. Then I couldn't resist pressing a kiss at the base of his throat. It was such a sweet little dip, exactly the size and shape where lips could press and linger.

His fingers slid up my spine, tightening in my hair. I savored the slight sting on my scalp because it distracted me from all my messy feelings.

"Nora," he murmured, his voice low and gravelly.

Gabriel was the only man whose voice could get to me. I'd never tested the theory, but I thought perhaps he could make me come just with his voice alone. It was rumbly and sexy and occasionally growly.

I *loved* it, like so much of him that I loved. My lips kept wandering, and I strung kisses along the line of his collarbone. His fingers tightened incrementally in my hair before he roughly tugged my head back. His eyes met mine, and the look there was pure fire. My insides went molten right before his mouth fit over mine. He claimed our kiss immediately with a bold sweep of his tongue.

Chapter Nine

GABRIEL

The feel of Nora pressed against me, warm and soft, and her tongue teasing with mine was a deep dive into sensation—fierce and undiluted pleasure. My senses were awash in her, and I drank her in like a starving man.

She moaned into our kiss, her fingers digging into the corded muscles along my spine when she pressed closer. I forced myself to gentle our kiss. Not because I wanted to. No, it was the opposite, in fact. But I needed to get it right with us this time.

It would be easy, *so* easy and so exquisitely tempting to let the desire that burned like an out-of-control brush fire between us take over. I knew how to give Nora what she wanted. I knew it thoroughly.

But letting that physical expression be what bound us together was what had led me in the wrong direction the first time with us. I gave a last glide of my tongue against hers before I pulled back, catching her bottom lip with my teeth lightly before releasing it. I cupped her cheek with my palm, letting my forehead fall to hers.

"I miss you, Nora." My lips moved against hers with every single word.

She made an inarticulate sound and then said, "I miss you too."

I clung to my control and forced my head to lift. I couldn't quite bring myself to step away fully yet. Her eyes blinked up at me, and I saw the vulnerability and uncertainty flickering there.

I hated myself for feeding into the doubts that I knew were woven deeply into her heart. I understood far too well why she had a hard time trusting others. The details were different, but her father had let her down time and again, just as my mother had let me down.

My heart twisted sharply as if I'd scored it with a knife, the blade jagged and dull. I'd done it myself— hurting her and hurting my own self. I thought I could never commit, and I'd thought she understood. She had at first. Then it got complicated because I'd been too stupid to realize I couldn't order my heart around the way I could the rest of my life.

"How do you know you love me?" Her voice was husky and throaty.

Her question felt like a punch to my gut. Not because she was trying to hurt me, but because it was so pointy, like a lance.

She had every right to ask me that. Hell, I'd told her I could never be serious. I'd even tried to argue the point and insist we could carry on as we had been. Friends with benefits. Friends who were special. I'd fucking said that. God, I'd been so fucking stupid.

"I don't know how I know. I just do," I said.

She blinked those liquid brown eyes, and I felt her take a breath. "I'm not going to be stupid again."

"What do you mean?" My heart was thudding in an unsteady, reckless beat.

"I fell for you, and I knew better. I don't want to get hurt again. I think maybe you think you love me because you miss me. But you miss what we had. Don't get me wrong, I know we have chemistry, and I know it's good with us. But good sex doesn't make for a good relationship."

"This isn't just about sex for me," I insisted.

I meant it, but I didn't know how to fight this fight with her. Because I'd never been in love. I was completely inexperienced and frankly stupid about love. The evidence of my foolishness hovered in the air around us, crossing like shadows over the sun in Nora's gaze. Doubts were emblazoned on her heart, and I'd put them there.

I smoothed her hair back, savoring the silky slide of it through my fingers. Every touch was something I was desperate for. "Give *us* a chance. Give *me* a chance."

"What happens next time? You were pretty clear about how you felt." Her lips twisted then, and I saw the pain flash in her eyes. I wished I had a million bandages to heal the wounds I'd created.

"It won't happen again."

She regarded me quietly. "I need to think."

"Okay. While you're thinking, I'll be waiting. Can we maybe have a truce in the meantime?"

"A truce?"

I felt my lips tugging at the corners. "One where you actually speak to me."

I saw the smile lurking in the corners of her mouth, but she didn't let it unfurl. "Okay. I'll stop giving you the silent treatment."

"Next time you need help with something, call me first."

Her nose wrinkled as she eyed me. "I didn't need help."

"Clearly, you did."

She finally laughed. "Okay, I did."

"I know you hate asking for help. You're the tomboy-est of the tomboys."

I couldn't resist smoothing a hand over her hair again as she looked up at me. "Not always."

"I know." My chest actually ached, and my eyes burned a little.

I wasn't prone to crying. Yet Nora, *only* Nora, brought emotion to the surface swiftly like this. Ever since I'd cut her off at the pass when she told me her feelings were more than just friends, whatever I'd buried deep inside after being abandoned by my mother and watching her flit in and out of our lives had roared to life. I couldn't tamp it down anymore.

Nora took a shaky breath, her grip finally easing as she shimmied out from between me and the counter, curling her arms around her waist tightly. "What are you doing this afternoon?" she asked.

"Helping you get the dryer hooked up," I prompted.

Her lips pressed in a tight line, and then she let loose a low laugh. "That would be nice."

Chapter Ten

GABRIEL

Flynn's sharp eyes held mine, studying me to the point I wanted to look away. I didn't.

Flynn was one of my best friends, solid as a rock. I'd used him as an excuse when I told Nora it was too complicated for us to have a relationship. With his gaze pinned on me, a sense of foreboding rose inside. I *knew* that Flynn knew. Hell, I was pretty sure he'd known all along, but he'd stayed quiet about it. Maybe not because of me, but probably Nora and her tendency to get real prickly when he interfered in her personal life.

"I noticed Nora is speaking to you again," he finally said.

After a long day of flying, circumstances worked out such that he and I were leaving to return to the resort from Diamond Creek at the same time. He suggested we grab dinner at Diamond Creek Brewery. It made no sense for me to refuse. Grabbing a beer with friends was perfectly normal, and Flynn and I had done it many times.

If I'd been wondering before, I knew now that he had an agenda other than food and drinks.

"Uh, yeah," I said slowly.

His lips twitched at the corners, and I sensed he was enjoying my discomfort. He took a bite of his burger, and I gratefully took that moment to enjoy a few fries. After he finished chewing, he cocked his head to the side and studied me quietly again.

"I knew something was up with you two. I only left it alone because I knew Nora would raise fucking hell with me if I interfered."

"How did you know?" I finally asked, resisting the urge to tap my fingers on the table.

In lieu of spinning my fork between my fingers because I tended to fidget when I was uncomfortable, I took a swallow of my beer, idly tracing my fingertip around the base of my glass after I set it down.

Flynn arched a brow, still watching me too perceptively for my comfort. "I'm not sure. It was more of a feeling. But then she stopped talking to you, so that pretty much said it all. What happened?" he asked, his tone cool.

It was only when he asked that question that I realized he might be pissed off at me or on the way to it. I figured the only thing on my side was Flynn was a controlled man. He was never impulsive, and he never flew off the handle. He could be a cranky ass, but falling in love with Daphne had softened his sharp edges.

I decided blunt honesty was my only option, or at least the only sensible option at the moment. I leaned back in the booth and ran a hand through my hair, not even bothering to hide my ragged sigh. "I fucked up is what happened. Now, I'm trying to fix it. Because I'm in love with Nora."

Flynn blinked, his eyes widening slightly. "You're in love with her?"

I nodded, a flash of defensiveness rising at the disbelief in his tone. "Yeah. It took her breaking things off for me to figure that out. Now, she doesn't believe me. She thinks I don't know what I'm talking about."

His gaze dipped down, and his shoulders shook. It took me a minute to realize he was silently laughing. At *me*.

When his eyes lifted, he shook his head slowly. "You're a fucking idiot. If you break her heart again, I'll kick your ass."

His laughter faded by that second sentence, and his icy blue gaze was lasered on me. My heart ached a little. Because I *was* a fucking idiot. Even worse, I *had* hurt Nora.

"I won't break her heart," I said firmly.

"Didn't you already?"

My chest burned. "I'm not sure. Look—" I began

Flynn shook his head. "You don't need to explain. As I said, I stayed out of it because Nora really doesn't appreciate it when I butt into her personal life. But you're my friend, and she's my sister. When I mentioned it to Daphne, she pointed out you were the one likely to get hurt this time. I didn't get it at first because I know how you are about relationships. That's your weakness."

I sighed again, running a hand through my hair before finishing off my beer. Setting the empty glass down, I rested my elbows on the table. "I guess so. She's pissed, and I don't know how to get her to believe I love her."

He shrugged. "Not gonna be easy. You know what my stepfather was like." Flynn's stepfather was Nora's father. I knew the sketch of their childhood, but not all of it. Flynn was nine years older than Nora, so I knew more of his version.

"Sort of," I offered, hoping Flynn might elucidate.

His lips tucked in at the corners, and I knew he was fighting back a smile. "Sure, I'll fill you in. It's no big secret. He was just a flake. My dad got our mom pregnant and then never showed up again. My stepdad was more of a bounce-in-and-out-of-our-lives kind of guy. Never really committing. Our mom was always waiting for him, and money was tight. Nora doesn't count on guys. Her not believing you is as much of a product of her father as it is you. I'm not sure what to tell you other than to be patient. She's going to expect you to walk away. It doesn't help matters that you already have."

"Fuck," I breathed. "You make it sound like I don't have a chance."

Flynn shrugged. "I didn't say that. Just remember: don't break her heart."

Chapter Eleven

NORA

"What do you need?" I called from the pantry.

I peered through the doorway of the pantry into the kitchen with a box of crackers in one hand. Daphne glanced over from where she was rinsing her hands by the sink. "Some clean dish towels, please."

"You got it, girl," I called as I turned around and reached for several dish towels from the stack we kept in here on the corner of one of the shelves.

Returning to the kitchen, I set the crackers down and swapped out the towels, tossing the used ones into the laundry bin we kept under one of the cabinets. "Need some help?" I asked as I leaned against the counter and opened the crackers.

I needed something to tide me over for the next few minutes until dinner. I'd meant to eat today, but it never happened because my flying schedule hadn't left me any time. As a result, I was hungry to the point of feeling faint.

Daphne smiled over at me as she turned off a burner. "No, but thank you."

She crossed over to the refrigerator. A moment later, she returned, handing me a tray of already sliced cheeses. "Sit down and eat before you fall over."

I did as she instructed. Rounding the counter, I slid my hips onto a stool and watched her get dinner ready for the staff while I nibbled on the cheese and crackers. I loved hanging out in the kitchen now. Ever since Daphne had taken over as chef here last year, the food was incredible, and she created a sense of warmth and welcoming. Previously, we'd gone through a series of cooks. Some were better than others, but it was more the practical matter of offering food to the guests. Flynn's prickly attitude and impatience had chased off a few, but he didn't dare mess with Daphne, so she made that better too.

Now, the guests were disappointed on the evenings when Daphne didn't serve a guest meal. She took two evenings off, and we encouraged the guests to go into town on those nights to take advantage of the local restaurants.

"How are things with Gabriel?" she asked after I finished my fourth cracker with a piece of cheese. Daphne did that often. She would strike with a targeted question just when you let down your guard.

I almost choked and held a finger up as I finished chewing. She handed me a glass of water, her eyes twinkling and her lips curled in a sly smile. I watched as she carefully shifted the seared vegetables from a pan onto a serving platter and drizzled some kind of sauce over them.

"What's that?" I asked after I finished chewing and took a sip of water.

"Vegetables with a lemon tarragon sauce. You didn't answer my question."

I sighed, glancing around furtively in case anyone was coming into the kitchen.

Daphne continued, "No one's here yet. Gabriel told Flynn he's in love with you."

"What?!" I sputtered.

Her eyes caught mine, her gaze somber as she nodded slowly. "Yes. I think he really means it."

Just then, my older brother came walking into the kitchen, calm and oblivious to our conversation. He stopped by Daphne, sliding his arms around her waist from behind and dipping his head to press a lingering kiss on the side of her neck.

Daphne's cheeks flushed pink. "Hi," she said, a little breathlessly.

I gave her an arch look. After confronting me about Gabriel and dropping that little bomb on me, she deserved to be embarrassed by my brother.

"Hey," Flynn said as he stepped away from Daphne. "I'm starving. Are you sharing?"

Before I could even answer, his long arm reached over to the counter where I sat opposite the stove and snagged one of my crackers with cheese.

"I guess I am," I said with a roll of my eyes.

I was torn about whether to confront Flynn about his conversation with Gabriel. Why was he even talking to Gabriel about me? I hated when he was nosy and overprotective. When Grant came walking through the back door, I decided I'd have to leave it alone. I didn't know if I should be furious at Flynn or Gabriel. No matter, I didn't appreciate them discussing me.

A few minutes later, Gabriel entered the kitchen and sat right beside me. That did it. I transferred my anger for him telling my brother about us directly and fully onto him. For fuck's sake. I couldn't believe he would talk to Flynn about us.

"How's it going?" Gabriel asked, oblivious to my state of mind.

That was a perfectly expected question. Nothing unusual about it at all. Except he spoke in that melodic, gravelly voice of his. I *loved* his voice. He could send shivers over my skin merely by speaking.

Perhaps it was because my nerves were already on edge, but the hairs rose on the back of my neck and along my forearms. I hadn't even looked at him yet.

Because my body was disobedient and oppositional when it came to Gabriel, my head turned automatically, my eyes whisking over to find his waiting. The moment I collided with his gaze, I felt struck by a jolt of electricity, firing every cell in my body. I swallowed and looked away, reaching for a cracker and stuffing it in my mouth. I could chew my feelings away. That was always effective.

"Can I have one?" he asked, his voice low.

I was so rattled, caught between anger and desire and the acute ache of missing him.

Sliding the plate between us, I nodded and looked away. That took an effort. Because I wanted to soak him in. I'd barely been able to stop thinking about him ever since he rescued me from my stupid washer situation.

He ate a few crackers with cheese, pausing afterward to take a long pull from a beer. Conversation carried on around us, the usual banter and friendly teasing.

"Are we not talking again?" Gabriel's words were just above a whisper, and only I could hear them.

Still, I looked around quickly, worried someone else would notice. Daphne and Cat were currently checking on something in the oven while Daphne explained something to Cat. Flynn was over by the table, joking around with Elias, who somehow appeared without me even noticing. Diego, Grant, and Tucker were debating the merits of two different types of beer from the local brewery.

My eyes arced over to the archway that led into the main area, where the guests often relaxed and mingled. A family was passing through, pulling on jackets as they walked out to the main entrance.

I finally gathered up the nerve to look into Gabriel's eyes again. It wasn't that I didn't want to. It was more that I was afraid of how much I *did* want to. "We're talking," I said, my tone almost mulish.

His eyes searched my face, and I resisted the urge to squirm in my seat. He knew me too well, too intimately, and I didn't like feeling so uncertain and vulnerable. And so needy, so very needy.

"That's good," he finally murmured.

I was beyond relieved when Elias's girlfriend, Cammie, appeared. "Hey!" I called the moment she came through the back door.

Her honey brown hair swung around her shoulders, her blue eyes lifting to mine with a smile. She held up a paper bag. "I brought wine since it's dinner. I'm not having any, but I figured you all might want some."

She stopped beside me at the corner of the counter, sliding several bottles of wine out of the bag and setting them there. Daphne crossed over as she dried her hands on a towel. "Oh, perfect. We can always use more wine. How come you're not having any?"

Cammi's cheeks went pink just as Elias came to Cammi's side, leaning over to give her a lingering kiss as he slid an arm around her waist. "Hey there."

She smiled up at him. It was no more than a blink of a moment, but the look that passed between them was so intimate, I had to look away. My heart ached, and my throat was tight. I wanted that. A man who loved me the way Elias loved Cammi.

When he lifted his head, Daphne cleared her throat. "Well?"

Cammi bit her lip and took a deep breath. "I'm pregnant."

Daphne squealed and clapped her hands.

Elias looked slightly puzzled. Cammi grinned up at him after she stepped back from a hug from Daphne. "I told you the guys wouldn't think it was a big deal."

"What do you mean?" Cat asked.

Cammi shrugged lightly. "Elias told Diego and Gabriel about it last week."

Laughter rumbled around us, and there were more congratulations. Somehow, I managed to chat casually with my friends and family. I was really happy for Elias and Cammi. *Really*. It wasn't as if I wanted an instant family. But it hurt to see how easily they'd fallen in love and how simple it was for them after that. It wasn't simple for me. Not at all.

My nerves were strung tight when Gabriel sat beside me at the table. I'd had good reasons for not talking to him. It had made it easier for me to hold on to my anger and not wish for more with him.

I didn't know what he thought he was doing, but I nearly jumped out of my chair when I felt his palm slide over my thigh in a soothing stroke. He reached for my hand and curled his around it. All of this took place under the table where no one could see.

I couldn't bring myself to shove his touch away. I craved it. His palm was warm around mine, and his thumb brushed in idle strokes along the sensitive skin on the inside of my wrist. Even worse, my emotions rose swiftly to the surface. Because it made me feel like he wanted me. It made me feel like maybe he did love me.

My righteous anger was slipping through my fingers, like sand caught in the wind and blown away.

Chapter Twelve

NORA

It was approaching eleven at night, and I was restless. After dinner, I'd escaped back to my place, thinking I needed something to distract me. Unfortunately, nothing was working. I'd flipped mindlessly through television channels, and I'd even taken a bath. Usually, a bath would help me wind down. Unfortunately, the only thing I could think of while I was in the tub was the last time I'd taken a bath with Gabriel. I'd been mastering the art of avoiding my memories of Gabriel over the past few months.

And for good reason, it seemed. Because all I could remember was the water sloshing over the edges of the tub when he pulled me over his lap. We'd been laughing. Now, the memory twisted sharp in my heart and left me aching and needy for him.

Don't be stupid, my smart mind ordered me.

That was the part of my brain that knew better. It had fed my anger and reminded my foolish heart why it had been so colossally stupid to fall for Gabriel in the first place.

There was another voice, perhaps the voice that I

had silenced for so long, long before Gabriel. The one that wanted me to think maybe not all men were flaky, unreliable assholes like my father.

He said he loved you. You know he's not a bad guy.

Maybe not, but he's the one who said he could never commit. How does he know it's different now?

It felt like a freaking tennis match in my brain. I was tired of it, and I couldn't seem to stem the relentless tide of desire that rushed through me, colliding with the tributary of my emotions. I was weary of trying to deny my want for him.

I didn't let myself think any further and leaned forward to scoop my phone off the coffee table.

Me: Come see me.

The second I fired off that text, my heart cast out rapid beats carelessly as anticipation spun inside. Somehow, it seemed by letting him back in, I was opening the door to my heart again. I was terrified, yet it was taking too much effort to keep that door closed. I felt as if I was still leaning my weight against the barricade I'd built to keep the wind of his presence out of my life. Yet he was with me in my heart all the time. He was also an undeniable physical presence in my life. I couldn't escape him or my feelings.

My phone vibrated seconds later.

Gabriel: On my way to you.

I didn't realize I'd been anxious about his reply until my relief rushed through me. Now, he couldn't get here fast enough.

Because I was *that* foolish about Gabriel, I stood and hurried into the bathroom. My hair was still damp and my cheeks still flushed from the bath. The locks were drying in tousled waves. I took stock of myself in the mirror. I considered myself the plainest of my siblings.

I'd inherited my father's brown hair and eyes. I studied myself, wondering just what Gabriel saw.

Annoyed at my ruminations, I splashed cold water on my face and was drying myself with a towel when I heard a sharp knock on the door. I practically ran out of the bathroom, forcing myself to slow my steps when I realized how much I was rushing.

The beat of my heart reverberated on repeat through my body when I stopped in front of the door. The knob felt cool under my palm, a contrast to the heat banked in my body. Just the knowledge that Gabriel was on the other side of the door fanned the flames. It was like air rushing into a closed space.

"I can hear you, you know?" Gabriel's voice reached me through the door, slightly muffled.

Hearing the hint of amusement in his tone, I almost giggled. I was being ridiculous.

I swung the door open. He stood there in the darkness. Only the light from inside my house cast over him. His lips barely curled up at one corner, sending my belly into wild flips.

"You didn't even turn on the light for me."

"I forgot."

"When you said you wanted me to come see you, did you mean for me to stand on the porch?"

The low timbre of his voice played on my nerves, already strung taut. I shook my head, stepping back to let him inside.

As he passed by, I picked up his scent, musky with a hint of spruce clinging to him. Closing the door behind him, I pressed my palms against the cool, wooden surface. He stopped just beyond the door, turning to face me. "Are we talking?"

I blinked before shaking my head. "I'd rather not."

My voice came out raspy, like torn velvet, ragged from the sharp edges of my need.

He closed the distance between us in two long strides. Resting his hands flat on the door, he caged me between his arms. His eyes skated over my face, dipping down and then back up.

My nipples perked up as if in greeting. It was only then I realized I was wearing a worn T-shirt with no bra. It was one of my favorite comfort shirts, and I didn't doubt he could see my body's reaction to his mere presence.

"It's important to me for you to understand how I feel," he said, each word slow and deliberate, his low voice caressing my nerves as his eyes bored into mine.

"What do you mean?" I rasped.

"I love you. I want a chance to get back to us."

My heart thrashed in my chest, and I felt a low tug in my belly. *Yes, yes, yes!* My foolish heart was falling for this man.

I knew I loved him, but I didn't know how to have faith that he loved me.

"Is it enough if I say I'll try to believe you?" I whispered.

Gabriel was quiet, and I started to feel a little panicky. I didn't want him to leave. I didn't want him to hold me at bay. And I knew how ridiculous that was, given that I hadn't spoken to him for months.

I needed him; I needed us. I needed the touchstone of our physical connection to remind me why it might be worth it to risk it all for him.

He closed his eyes, leaning his head back as he took a deep breath. When he leveled his gaze with mine again, the look there was so intense it took my breath away. Mind you, between the wild rush of my heartbeat, my breath was shallow to begin with.

"I'm trying to tell myself that we need to take it slow," he murmured.

I finally took one of my palms away from the door, placing it on his chest over his heart, simultaneously reassured and excited by the rapid thump of it.

"I need you."

The words fell between us. I meant them. Completely. Those three words were insufficient to capture the depth and breadth of my need for Gabriel at this moment.

"Okay," he whispered.

Then I watched as he moved slowly, almost as if he was giving me a chance to change my mind. No way in *hell* was that happening.

He lifted a hand, lightly brushing his knuckles across the line of my cheekbone. His touch traveled, tracing one of my brows and then moving up along my hairline as he smoothed a loose lock of hair off my cheek. The feel of his fingers brushing over the shell of my ear as he tucked the hair behind it sent fire racing over the surface of my skin.

"Please." My request came in a husky whisper.

He granted my wish. His lips brushed mine once and then again. I heard the reverberation of his low groan against my palm where it was still pressed over his heart. He finally gave me what I wanted, what I craved—a commanding, devouring kiss as he fit his mouth fully over mine.

I was arching into him, moaning shamelessly into our kiss as I wound my arms around his neck. He lifted me high against him, bringing me with such ease into his strong hold.

Not many men could make me feel the way Gabriel did—as if he could wrap me into his embrace and protect me and shelter me from anything that came my way.

I'd never known I craved that feeling until him. My heart shouted out cheers, and my body surrendered to the roar of desire, a wild cacophony between us.

I didn't even realize I'd wound my legs around his waist until I felt the hard press of his arousal against me. I was already drenched with need, and my core clenched at the feel and awareness of his response. I was restless. When he drew away, I curled a palm around the back of his head and murmured, "More."

His low chuckle sent sparks skating over the surface of my skin. I felt prickly all over, so frantic for him that I spurred my heels into his muscled ass.

"You asked for me, and you've got me, darling, but I am *not* rushing this. I've waited too long for you."

Still holding me, he turned and angled over to the side of the room. In another moment, he was carrying me easily up the stairs. Impatient, I nipped at his neck, murmuring, "It's only been four months."

"You're only counting since you cut me off. I'm dialing back to when I first knew how much I wanted you."

Gabriel crested the top stair. That comment got my attention, and I lifted my head from the mouthwatering taste of his skin. He crossed the upstairs landing into my bedroom as I asked, "What do you mean?"

He wasn't looking at me as he crossed the room. I didn't think he was avoiding my gaze, considering he was carrying me. There was no need to collide with furniture on the way. He was a far too practical man for that kind of fumble.

A moment later, he eased me down on the bed, resting his palms on either side of me on the mattress as he looked into my eyes. "I suppose if I want you to believe I love you, I could start with telling the truth. I wanted you the first time I met you."

I blinked. "Five years ago?"

He nodded slowly and deliberately. "It didn't seem smart to make a move on the little sister of one of my best friends the very first day I moved here to work for him."

My thoughts scrambled to align around this detail. Gabriel had never mentioned this before. He played it off over the past year when we started sneaking around. He made it seem like a new thing for him. In all honesty, it *had* been a new thing for me.

I was dumbfounded, and it must have shown on my face because Gabriel lifted one shoulder in a light shrug. "True story."

My heartbeat stuttered, catching and then taking off in a thundering beat as we stared at each other. "Oh," I breathed.

"Oh." A teasing, wicked glint entered his eyes, and his lips curled in a belly spinning, sensual smile.

Then he was kissing me again, and I fell into the flood of need, caught in a current of raw desire, rushing like a river overflowing. His tongue tangled with mine as I felt his weight shift when he lifted a hand off the mattress, cupping my breast through my T-shirt. He thumbed my nipple, and the sensation of his touch with the fabric lightly abrading my skin had me crying out into his mouth. He lifted his head, standing abruptly.

I whimpered, feeling bereft to have him move away from me. With one hand, Gabriel hooked the hem of his T-shirt and dragged it up and over his head. When he tossed it aside, it fell in a whispering rumple to the floor. Greedy for him, I stretched my hand out, trailing my fingers over his muscled abdomen. He had a lean, rangy build. On the tall side, topping six feet, two inches, he had broad shoulders and arms corded with muscles. There was a light dusting of auburn hair on his chest and a teasing trail that disappeared behind his waistband.

My fingers immediately reached for the buttons on his fly, and he caught one of my hands in his warm grip. "Slow your roll, darling."

Biting my lip, I cast a glare up at him. He replied by palming my cheek and leaning down to catch my lips in a fierce kiss. He had my clothes off in record time, throwing my T-shirt aside and lifting me from the bed to shove my sweatpants down around my hips. I shimmied and kicked them free. This time, he didn't stop me when I reached for his fly.

With an assist from him, his jeans were kicked loose, and I sighed as I stroked my palm over the swollen length of his cock. When I moved to push his fitted briefs down, he shook his head, pressing his palm to my chest and levering me backward on the bed.

"Not yet. I need something to help me stay in control."

"You're always in control, you—" My protest died in a gasp when his mouth captured one of my nipples, sucking just hard enough that a piercing shot of plea-sure arrowed from there straight to my core, which clenched in rippling reply.

"You're always—" My breath hissed through my teeth when his lips closed over my other nipple, and his touch moved lightly over my belly before I felt his fingers teasing over the damp cotton of my panties.

"I'm always what?" he murmured as he grazed his teeth over my nipple, the feel of his lips on my skin sending another spasm of pleasure through me.

"In control," I gasped out.

He lifted his head. "Look at me."

It took an effort, but I opened my eyes, the lids heavy as I stared at him. "With you, I'm almost never in control. And it's been four months and six days and thirteen hours since I was last with you like this."

My heart thrashed violently in my chest. "You've been counting?" My question was a raspy whisper.

"To the minute." He glanced at his watch. His tone was solemn as his eyes bored into mine. "Remember? I had to leave early that day to go to Anchorage. We had a fight, and you told me to go."

I swallowed as a rush of emotion spun into the pulse of need pounding through me. "Oh," was all I could muster.

In another moment, he brought his lips to mine as he pushed the cotton out of the way and teased his fingers through my slippery wet folds. My entire body was pulsing, swollen and achy with need. My sex clenched when he slipped two fingers into me.

Cast adrift in the current of need and caught in the intensity of finally being with him after too long, I was relieved there was no more talking. I needed this, needed him as much as I needed air to breathe.

Gabriel's lips teased, kindling my body with light nips on my neck, a piercing suck on one nipple as he pinched the other. He blazed a trail of fiery kisses over my belly. One of his palms slid up the inside of my thigh, the firm pressure something for me to hold on to as sensation threatened to spin me loose.

I felt the pressure of his shoulders between my thighs and then his fingers sinking into me again as his thumb teased over my swollen and aching clit. I was frantic, pleading for more, chasing after a sweet surrender I knew would come like a wave crashing on the shore.

He licked into my folds, teasing me with his tongue and his fingers as the fire inside kindled hotter and hotter, the flames rushing through me. I was gasping, crying as the pressure drew so tight in my center I thought I might shatter.

But Gabriel wouldn't let that happen. When the pressure finally did break loose, I cried out in exquisite ecstasy, and he held me together with soothing strokes of his palms as he rose over me. He hooked one of my knees around his elbow and then filled me in one deep stroke, seating himself deeply as my climax still rippled.

"Nora," he whispered in a gruff command.

When I opened my eyes, I was ensnared instantly in his gaze, the gold flecks in his green eyes like embers of fire. My heart thumped hard, in tune with his as his weight came down over me.

Maybe I could believe he loved me. Just thinking that felt so dangerous I was relieved when his lips claimed mine, and he drew back before filling me once again.

Chapter Thirteen

GABRIEL

"Nora." Her name came out slurred, my voice thickened with the intense sensation of being inside her again. The relief of being joined with her was so powerful, my entire body hummed in pleasure.

Her silky, clenching core stroked and rippled around me as her hips rose to meet my every stroke. Her skin was damp, and there was a wildness to her, an abandon I hadn't felt from her before.

My own release was already threatening, electricity sizzling at the base of my spine as my balls felt heavy, drawing tight against my body when I sank into her yet again. I reached between us, resting my weight on one elbow as I found her swollen bud.

"I can't come again," she murmured in a ragged gasp.

I held still, staring into her passion-drowsed gaze. "Come for me."

I clung to my control, so, *so* close to the edge of my release. I dipped my head and pressed kisses along the side of her neck. I nipped at her earlobe, savoring when she arched into me like a cat, letting out a ragged whimper.

I teased my fingers in a slow circle where we were joined, glancing over her. I felt it when she trembled and rippled around my shaft.

"That's my girl," I murmured when she moaned.

My name was a tattered cry, and I felt her climax coming. Drawing my hips back, I slid into her again, savoring her keening cry as I shuddered. I finally let go, my release breaking as if a dam had been opened, crashing through me so hard I lost my breath.

It was all over then, but for the feeling of being cast ashore after a storm as I fell against her. Rolling quickly to my side, I wasn't ready to lose our connection, so I was relieved when she rolled with me. Straddling me, she rested against my chest, and I could feel the warm gusts of her breath against my shoulder.

My heart was stumbling in my chest, emotion threatening to overtake me. I'd come to terms with my heart—I loved Nora, and I didn't want to lose her again. Yet even facing that truth hadn't prepared me for how it would feel to be intimate with her when I knew it.

I'd meant what I said earlier when she said I was always in control. I'd never been in control with her, yet I'd been able to fool myself into thinking I was. She'd slipped through the walls I'd built around my heart, and now they were nothing but piles of broken kindling. I felt exposed and raw and was relieved she didn't seem inclined to talk at the moment. All the same, I would've been devastated if she were to pull away.

I slid my fingers through her silky hair, my heartbeat gradually slowing, and a sense of calm settling inside me, finally. When I felt her lift her head, I thought I was prepared, that I wouldn't let the tears that had threatened moments earlier take over. I wasn't a man who cried easily. Perhaps I'd known if I ever fell it would be hard to keep the depth of my emotion at bay. Nothing could've prepared me for this, though.

She rose up, and I opened my eyes, shifting slightly to prop some pillows behind my back with one arm. Sitting astride me, she looked like an earthy angel. Her dark hair was falling around her shoulders, half covering one of her breasts. Her lips were kiss-swollen and pink, and her dark eyes, like rich espresso, blinked at me.

We stared at each other, and my heart began to kick hard again, making a racket in my chest. I saw a worried flicker in her eyes, and I hated it, hated the hurt she carried. Most of all, I hated that I actually added to the hurt she already held inside. I let my hands slide down her sides, then over the sweet dip of her waist.

"I love you."

She blinked again, her eyes going wide and her breath catching in a startled hitch in her throat. Her eyes flicked down, and she spread her palm on my chest. I knew she could feel the unsettled rhythm of my heart under her touch, and I didn't care.

When her lashes lifted again, she looked bashful. "I'm not ready to say that," she said carefully.

"I know," I whispered.

What she said next surprised me. "But I feel it."

We regarded each other quietly, and I slid my hands up her waist again and back down to rest on the silky smooth skin of her thighs. "Can I stay tonight?"

When she nodded, I felt as if I'd won something big. Yet I knew this was only the beginning of proving her wrong, proving she could trust me now when she couldn't before.

Chapter Fourteen

NORA

Flynn stood at the kitchen counter, eating cheese like everything was perfectly fine. I had to admit, even though I loathed to do so, my mood was better after my night with Gabriel several days prior.

I hadn't planned it that way, but it turned out I needed to go to Anchorage for several days to run errands for the resort and pick up some construction materials. We had this idea to build a viewing platform near the main lodge where moose and other wildlife often passed through.

When I heard my brother Grant grumbling about needing to go, I jumped on it. As much as I'd savored my night with Gabriel, I was bordering on panic. Finding an excuse to be out of town for a few days bought me some time to gather myself emotionally.

Unfortunately, that time also freed me to stew over Flynn saying something to Gabriel about us. My mind replayed my conversation with Gabriel the following morning, yet again.

"He told you what?" I'd asked.

Gabriel eyed me, and I hadn't missed the cautious

look in his gaze. "He's the one who asked me about you. You know I wouldn't say anything if he hadn't. I couldn't exactly lie. He's my friend, and you're his sister."

As I'd stared at him, I felt caught between my conflicting impulses. All this time, we'd tried to keep our friends-with-benefits arrangement private. I was the one who'd demanded my family not know about it. Yet when I'd told Gabriel I wanted more, he was the one who said he didn't want to screw up his friendship with Flynn. He'd claimed it was too complicated. That was only one of his excuses. The other was that he could never be serious. It just wasn't something he could do, or so he'd said.

A part of me wanted Gabriel to want to talk to Flynn. For his feelings for me to be so powerful that he had to break down and tell him. Yet my strongly ingrained need for privacy rose up forcefully. The need to control what my brother knew about my personal life.

I'd looked up to Flynn for my entire childhood. After our mother passed and he came home, I'd been a teenager awash in a confusing jumble of grief and anger. To have him show up and basically function as a father had been hard on us both. Both of us could be stubborn. Years had passed since then, and I felt differently. With maturity and context, I could look back and laugh a little at how much we'd clashed. Now, we could even joke that I'd been his practice for Cat.

"You're gonna break that coffee mug if you keep holding on to it that hard." Flynn's voice broke into my train of thought.

I glanced at my hand to see my knuckles were white where they curled around the mug. I lifted my eyes to his and shrugged. I eased the tight curl of my fingers and set the mug on the counter. I opened my mouth to speak before pausing and glancing around. The kitchen at the resort was the heartbeat of this place as far as staff went. At any given moment, any one of our friends or family members could come traipsing through here. Considering my feathers had been ruffled over Flynn's intrusion into my privacy, I didn't want to deal with someone else appearing in the middle of this conversation.

Nothing but quiet reached my ears, so I turned back to Flynn. "Why the hell did you talk to Gabriel about me?"

My brother held my gaze steadily. With a subtle quirk of a brow, he shrugged. "Because I felt like it. I don't want you to get hurt."

Anger and defensiveness twisted inside my chest. "I can take care of myself, Flynn. I don't need you interfering in my life."

"Interfere? What the fuck, Nora? You're my sister, and Gabriel is my friend. I'm not trying to get in the middle. I'm just not sure I trust him not to hurt you. He already has."

"He's one of your closest friends. How can you say you don't trust him?" I wrapped my arms around my waist, gripping my elbows.

"Oh, I trust him, generally speaking. He's just not known for making a commitment. To anyone. You haven't spoken to him in months. Which, I have to say, has been impressive," he offered dryly.

Unbothered by my anger, he snagged another slice of cheese off the tray sitting on the counter, waiting calmly for my reply.

I hated how calm Flynn was. He was always calm. The only time he wasn't was when it came to Daphne. I resented his calmness, and I didn't like admitting it, but a tiny corner of my heart was envious of what he had with Daphne.

As the oldest, Flynn had always seemed removed from the chaos my father created for Grant, Cat, and me. He was Flynn's stepfather, and so somehow, Flynn seemed separated from the emotional tumult. By the time I was old enough to think more clearly about my father, Flynn was off in the Air Force. Then he reappeared after our mom died, the one stable force in our lives. Thick in the midst of my grief over her loss, I'd had to deal with my annoyingly calm and steady older brother. We'd clashed for a while with things finally settling down in the past couple of years.

"I can take care of myself," I muttered, feeling the heat burning on my cheeks.

"I know you can take care of yourself, Nora," Flynn returned, still freaking calm. "I'm assuming if your feelings weren't hurt, you would've actually been speaking with Gabriel these last few months. What happened anyway?"

"How do you know anything happened?"

My brother raised his eyes to the ceiling, letting out a slow, controlled breath as he leveled his gaze with mine again. "I'm not stupid, Nora. Maybe I didn't pick up on it right away, but I eventually gathered you two had some kind of arrangement. I didn't talk with anybody other than Daphne about it because I know how insanely private you are. I didn't want it to turn into an argument between us. Then you stopped talking to him. Now, you're talking to him again. Maybe I'm missing most of the details, but I can deduce that something happened."

"So what?" I grumbled, annoyed by how perceptive he could be. Although I supposed it didn't take a rocket scientist to notice something was up with Gabriel and me.

"Just tell me what happened, Nora," he pressed.

"Nothing. I don't want to talk about it."

"Well, then why the hell did you start this conversation?" Flynn retorted, narrowing his eyes.

"Because I didn't appreciate you saying something to Gabriel about us, which tells me that you had a conversation with him about it."

At that moment, as bad luck would have it, my brother Grant came walking in the kitchen from the back hallway. His alert gaze landed on Flynn and me immediately, bouncing between us before he stopped beside Flynn, eyeing me warily.

Grant was a slightly younger version of Flynn. They shared the same dark blond hair and glacial blue eyes. Grant was a little lankier in build and a more easy-going guy than Flynn. He was always quick with a smile and a quip.

"What's up?" he asked.

"Nothing," I mumbled, tightening my arms around my waist.

"Uh, okay."

Flynn, because he was an overbearing ass sometimes, offered, "Nora is pissed at me because I asked Gabriel about them."

Grant pursed his lips and nodded slowly. "Oh," was all he had to offer in response.

"Don't you dare talk to Gabriel too," I said.

Grant glanced back at me. "I wasn't planning to. I mean, I'll kick his ass if he hurts you, but otherwise, I'll leave it be."

"Oh, my God," I muttered as I turned and stomped out of the kitchen.

I crossed through the main room at the resort,

angling over to the staircase and jogging up it quickly. I'd come over here for the yoga class. Last summer, we made arrangements for Gemma, a local yoga teacher, to come out once a week to teach a class to the guests. She also held one for the staff afterward. I walked along the wide hallway on the upper floor, passing the rows of doors that led into the guest rooms, slowing as I approached the rec room she used for her classes at the end of the hall.

Her soothing voice carried out to me in the hallway. Leaning my back against the wall, I slid my hips down to the floor and rested my forehead on my knees.

"Now, let's start with one full breath. Breathe in through your nose, come up slowly and bring your breath all the way into your belly. Count to four and hold. One, two, three, four. Now, let your breath go on the count of four, three, two, one," Gemma said to the class.

I breathed along with her instructions from the hall, trying to ease the anger and frustration spinning inside me. I hated knowing that Flynn was right. Obviously, I'd stopped speaking to Gabriel for a reason. Obviously, Gabriel still had the capacity to hurt me.

Yet I wanted him too much to keep him at bay.

At the sound of light footsteps approaching, I lifted my forehead from my knees, looking down the hall to see Daphne walking toward me.

She stopped in front of me, her perceptive gaze skimming my face quickly before she turned and slid her hips down the wall to sit beside me, mirroring my pose with her knees pulled up. She rested her chin on her hands folded over her knees and angled her face to look at me.

"What's up?"

Daphne had this way about her. When she first arrived at Walker Adventures as a guest last year, I'd liked her immediately, although she came across as rather buttoned up and prissy, even prim at times. As I'd gotten to know her, I'd discovered she was fiercely loyal and kind, and she had a silly side that only came out around those who knew her well. She'd been through her own trial by fire when she lost her son to a rare form of brain cancer when he was only five years old. In spite of that, or perhaps because of it, she tended to charge at life, and she held those close to her in her embrace and was fiercely protective.

Flynn had fallen for her so hard, my poor brother had scared himself. I trusted no one more than Daphne to protect his heart the way she did. Her gaze contained a tender gravity, and I knew she would understand.

"Flynn and I had an argument. It might've been my fault," I mumbled.

She blinked, her lips curling very slightly in a smile. "Or perhaps it was his fault. He does have that kind of —" Lifting her chin off her hands, she gave an airy wave. "You know, like a brother-knows-best kind of vibe. With me, it's man-knows-best, and it can be annoying. Did you want to slap him? Happens to me now and then. Although I would never do that."

A laugh rustled in my throat, and I leaned back against the wall, straightening my legs and rolling my ankles in circles. "I know you wouldn't. He does know best, or he likes to think so. I didn't appreciate him talking with Gabriel about us."

"Ah," she said with a sage nod. "I advised him against that. He said he felt it was necessary because he didn't want Gabriel to be stupid."

"Stupid?"

"Yeah, by breaking your heart again. If he did that, Flynn would be caught in the middle. He doesn't want to make a choice between you and one of his best friends," Daphne said matter-of-factly. She straightened her legs as well and removed an elastic hairband from her wrist. She continued talking while she slipped her fingers through her hair and twisted it into a ponytail. "Flynn loves you, and he's worried that you and Gabriel sort of share similar baggage."

I groaned and leaned my head against the wall behind me. "Great. So he's talked to you about this too?"

She divided the ponytail and gave it a tug to tighten it. Dropping her hands, she looked at me again. "Of course. He tells me everything. He does have enough sense to know I won't tell him everything you tell me, though."

Shifting close to her, I wrapped my arm around her shoulder and gave her a squeeze before leaning back again. "You're the best almost-sister-in-law I could have."

Her cheeks went a little pink. "Same."

"How about we discuss when you and Flynn are actually going to get married?" I teased lightly.

Daphne's cheeks flushed even pinker. "I don't know. I haven't had time to plan it."

"Well, we need to get to planning for Cammi and Elias."

"Oh, I know," she said slowly. "I am so happy for them."

"Elias is so much more mellow these days," I commented.

"Regular sex will do that," Daphne offered frankly just as the door to the yoga room opened.

Gemma glanced down at us, her lips twitching with a smile. "Agreed."

We burst into laughter as we stood. We waited while the guests left the room and then walked in. I put my shoes away in one of the little cubbies Cat had set up. We all had our own yoga mats now.

Gemma's honey-gold curls glinted under the late afternoon sunlight falling through the front windows. The days were getting shorter as we moved into autumn, but we still had sunshine in the evening for now.

"How many staff do you think will be here tonight?" Gemma asked as Daphne and I took our favorite spots off to one side in the front.

"Almost everyone showed up last week. Will Diego be here?" I asked.

Gemma shrugged. "I think so."

Daphne laughed at my side. She was bent at the waist, her hands resting on the floor as she stretched her back, so her voice was muffled as she spoke. "Of course, he'll be here. Then he'll go home with Gemma. We're gonna have to find another person to take his room."

"Do you think Harley will stay?" I asked as Daphne straightened. I was referring to Diego's little sister, Harley, who'd come to stay in the staff house a few months ago and had extended her stay several times since.

Daphne shrugged. "You know as much as me. Of course, she's welcome to stay as long as she'd like. She's been helping out with the website and everything."

"I know. She's made it look great. What do you know?" I asked, looking at Gemma.

Diego, one of the pilots here, had recently fallen for Gemma. "I'm not sure either. I don't think Harley really has any plans, and her work is all online, so it works out for her to stay here."

"Is she falling for someone here?" Daphne asked, looking around the room.

Gemma snorted a laugh. "I don't know."

As if conjured by our conversation, Diego came strolling through the door with Harley right behind him. He crossed straight to Gemma, stopping in front of her and running his hands lightly from her shoulders down to her elbows as he leaned down and pressed a kiss on her temple.

It felt as if we were interrupting a suddenly intimate moment. Harley called over, "Cut the PDA, y'all."

Diego stepped back and cast a lingering smile at Gemma. The warmth and possessiveness in his eyes sent a ping through my chest. Lately, it seemed I was watching all of my friends fall in love and wishing I could have something like it.

Diego crossed the room to fetch his yoga mat and put his shoes in a cubby while Harley walked briskly over to unroll her mat beside Daphne. She smiled over at us. "Don't get me wrong, I love that my brother's in love. But really. Some of us—" She cut her words off abruptly when Diego stopped beside her.

"Some of us, what?" he prompted as he unrolled his yoga mat.

"Nothing," Harley replied airily.

I felt a prickle on the back of my neck that raced down my spine, and I knew Gabriel had arrived. Great, just great. I'd come to yoga class to relax, and now I would be a ball of tension because *he* was here.

Too late, I realized there was room for someone on my other side. In a matter of seconds, he was there.

"Hey, Nora." His voice was low, and even though

others were around, it felt as if we were alone. His tone was warm and intimate, sending butterflies into flight in my belly and tingles chasing through my body. I'd had that unsettling and confusing reaction to him ever since we'd given in to the chemistry that sparked between us.

I was so easily turned on by him, my nerves firing and sending signals of passion and need through me. It wasn't solely that, though. My heart felt a visceral tug toward him.

GABRIEL

"Hell, yeah!" Diego said, raising a fist in the air as he laid down a winning hand on the coffee table with his free hand.

Flynn, who often won, simply grinned and pushed the small pile of coins across the table to Diego.

Seconds later, he was collecting cards and shuffling them for another round. I leaned back into the couch cushions, rolling my achy shoulder. "Can you grab me a beer?" I called when Grant stood and walked into the kitchen.

We were at the staff house, a house we'd built two summers prior. Once the resort had gotten busy, it was clear the staff needed somewhere else to stay other than occupying needed guest rooms. These days, I lived here with Grant, Tucker, and Harley, Diego's younger sister. Lately, Diego was mostly over at Gemma's.

It was almost amusing—*almost*—that I'd been teasing my friends about falling in love, thinking all along that I would never fall. Now, I had to convince Nora to believe me.

I rolled my head along the back of the couch, catching Diego's eyes. "When are you going to call it official?"

"Call what official?" he countered.

Grant returned to the room, handing me a bottle of beer. I took a long pull as Flynn answered Diego's question for me. "Move in with Gemma and get married," he teased.

"Yeah," Grant interjected. "You're not drinking tonight because you have to drive out there. When's the last time you stayed out here anyway?"

At that moment, the front door opened, and Elias peered around it. "Hey, guys. Daphne said I'd find you over here. Sorry I missed dinner." He walked in, closing the door behind him. "I was going to bring coffee, but coffee isn't usually what we do for card night," he explained as he hung his jacket on the hooks by the door and toed his boots off. "I brought this instead." He held up two growlers from the local brewery.

"Smart move," Flynn said with a chuckle. "Want in on the game?"

"He can have my hand," I offered. "I'm on a losing streak tonight. Maybe you can improve for me."

Elias laughed as he sat down beside me. "I'll do my best. Oh crap, I need to put these in the refrigerator."

Grant hadn't sat back down yet and offered, "I got 'em." He snagged the two growlers with one hand and crossed over to put them in the refrigerator in the kitchen.

The lower floor of this house was comprised of a large living room with a woodstove to one side and a kitchen at the back, along with a combined bathroom and laundry room. Four bedrooms and two full baths were upstairs. It was pretty comfy for the staff and didn't cost us a penny to live here.

"I was wondering if you and Cammi would be here for dinner tonight," I commented as I glanced at Elias.

"I meant to make it, but I was running a little late. We're wedding planning." His eyes went a little wide at that.

Diego smiled and thumped his fist over his heart. "Smart man."

"Are you panicking yet?" Flynn teased as he lifted his cards and organized them in his hand.

Elias shook his head, his lips twitching with a slight smile. "Nah." His tone was almost wondering. "I kind of can't believe it."

"When it's right, it's right," Diego commented.

"Speaking of right, are you still trying to keep up the façade that you live out here?" Elias quipped.

Diego's teeth flashed with his quick grin. "I'm not pretending. Just gotta get around to moving everything. Where is Harley, by the way?" he asked, referring to his younger sister.

"No clue," I replied with a shrug.

"I think she said she was going into town to Sally's," Grant offered when he sat down on the sectional couch near Flynn.

Diego glanced at Grant. "I think she might be seeing somebody and doesn't want me to know."

"Is she supposed to let you know?" I asked, genuinely curious.

"No, but she damn sure thinks I'm supposed to tell her everything about Gemma and me," he deadpanned.

I felt Flynn's gaze on me. When I looked up, he held my eyes for a few beats. I resisted the urge to look away. I knew he was trying to give me a clear chance to get it right with his sister this time. As much as I had faith in my feelings, I had plenty of doubts about myself. Trying to navigate being in love was like being tossed onto the shores of a new land where no one spoke my language.

I took a swallow of my beer and leaned back. Flynn was the reason I was here tonight. I'd wanted to go to Nora's after dinner at the resort, but I was usually here when we had a casual game of cards. I promised myself I wasn't going to lie and sneak around this time, so here I was.

Elias actually managed to win the next game with my hand. We chatted about his upcoming wedding and the news that Cammi was pregnant with twins. Everything had changed for him lightning fast. I kept thinking if he could go from being a bachelor who'd eschewed commitment to a man who embraced the love of his life and looked forward to having a family, then I could too.

I forced my thoughts off Nora. I swear, the woman had a dedicated track in my mind, like a train circling on a loop. It was always good to hang out with my friends, and I'd rather enjoy it than dwell on trying to figure out this thing with Nora and me—this knot I couldn't untangle.

Later, after Flynn left to return to the resort, Elias departed to head home with Diego following him to town as well, and Tucker went upstairs to bed, I decided to slip away to see Nora. I forced myself to text her first.

Me: Now?

My heartbeat echoed in my ears as I waited for her response. I was impatient, but I wanted to get this right. I wanted to see her so badly, my body nearly ached with the force of my need.

Nora: Now sounds good.

Her reply came far too many minutes later.

———

A quick jog through the crisp autumn air had my entire body feeling alive. Frost was forming on the ground and fallen leaves and evergreen needles crunched under my feet as I moved along the path from the staff house to her place.

The porch light cast a warm glow in the darkness, and my heart kicked in my chest as I climbed the steps to her door, knocking lightly.

"Come in!" her voice was muffled through the door.

I was unaccustomed to this sense of being wound tight. I'd been holding my emotions at bay for so long. Now that I'd let myself actually *feel* in my fight to get back to us, there was another layer to my feelings— running more deeply and fiercely.

The doorknob was cool under my palm as I turned it. Stepping through, I closed it behind me. Nora was standing in the kitchen across the room. Her hair was pulled up in a messy ponytail. I kicked off my shoes and crossed the room to her as she turned to face me.

"Hey." I stopped in front of her, resting my hands on her upper arms, needing the contact to anchor me in the tumult of emotions storming through me.

Her thick lashes lifted, and her brown eyes skimmed over my face. "Hey," she said softly, her voice a little raspy.

"Now is good?" I asked, referencing her reply to my text.

She canted her head to the side, biting the corner

of her lip. The sight of her white teeth denting the smooth pink surface of her lips made me a little crazy.

"I think so."

"You think?"

She released her lip and let out a little puff of a breath. "Yes, now is good."

"Perfect," I murmured.

I slid my hands down, curling them around her hips, savoring her soft curves as I lifted her and slipped her bottom onto the counter. She let out a startled gasp as I tugged her close to the edge and stepped between her knees. I took the moment to simply look at her, to soak her in.

I loved Nora's contrasts. She was such a tomboy. She flew planes with ease and grace, she didn't blink at life in the wilderness in Alaska, a sometimes unforgiving and harsh land. Yet, she was so feminine. Her dark brows arched delicately, and her nose turned up at the end. Her lips made a perfect pink bow. Her curves were soft, thoroughly generous.

I stepped closer, feeling the heat of her against my arousal. I had it that bad for Nora. The moment I knew I was going to be able to be with her, I was swollen with need for her.

I dipped my head, dusting a kiss on the underside of her jaw, feeling the wild throb of her pulse there.

"Gabriel?" she whispered, a lilt of a question in her tone.

"Mmm?" I murmured as I trailed my tongue along the sensitive shell of her ear, loving her subtle shiver.

"What are you doing?" The rasp in her voice sent a sizzle of need through my body.

"You said now was good. I took that literally."

"Oh."

I lifted my head. "You know how literal I am."

Her eyes sparkled, and she bit her lip again. "You are. We could go to the bedroom," she offered.

"We could, but I like the kitchen. You know that too."

Pink bloomed on her cheeks, and her chocolate eyes darkened. "I like the kitchen too," she murmured.

In all honesty, when it came to Nora, it wasn't a place or time. It was *her*. Only she had the ability to set me on fire and catch my heart in the net of sparks created by the fire. Only *she* held my heart in her hands, and I never wanted her to let it go.

"What's this?" I asked, my voice husky as I caught the strap of her overalls between two fingers and trailed my fingers down along that strip of fabric. I paused when I felt her nipple tighten behind my knuckles when they grazed over it.

I couldn't resist dipping my head and dusting a kiss over the soft skin where her pulse beat rapidly. Her breath hissed through her teeth, and she let out a little whimper on her exhale.

"You haven't answered me," I murmured against her skin, pushing the strap of her overalls out of the way and cupping her breast. The weight of it was lush and full in my palm.

"I forgot your question," she gasped, her breath tattered.

Lifting my head, I clarified, "I suppose I didn't explain. Why are you wearing overalls at home? They're not convenient. Tsk, tsk."

Nora giggled, and the sound went straight to my heart, sending a sharp, piercing shock to it. She didn't giggle often. She was a very practical girl, and I loved that about her. But her intense practical nature meant that she only giggled when she really let down her guard. Sprouts of hope shot up in my heart.

Maybe I could persuade her to believe I loved her. Maybe I could rebuild what I'd sent up in flames when I tried to keep my feelings for her at bay.

"I didn't know you were coming over, and I haven't changed since I got home," she explained.

I leaned back, letting my eyes coast over her. Her breasts rose and fell along with her rapid breath. Her pupils were dilated, and her eyes dark as espresso. I released a put-upon sigh.

"Well, let's take care of these then."

She let out a surprised laugh when I lifted her from the counter to set her on her feet in front of me. I immediately shoved down her overalls, pushing them over her hips where they fell in a denim rumple on the floor. She kicked them free of her feet. When I looked down, I noticed she was wearing bright yellow socks, like little splashes of sunshine in the room.

Impatience spurred me, and I slid my palms over the sweet curves of her hips and under the hem of her T-shirt, letting it ride up my wrists as I pushed it up over her head. I lingered for a moment to tease her breasts.

There was a whooshing sound as we freed her T-shirt and tossed it on the floor. She stood in front of me in a pair of practical cotton panties with a cream silk bra. Matching was not my girl's thing.

I wanted to take it slow, to drag this out, but I needed her too badly. That was something else only Nora could do. She always had me grasping to maintain my control. Even when I wanted to play a seductive game to orchestrate her pleasure, it never worked out that way. It was a mad rush, like getting tossed into a river current I could not swim against.

She rested a hand on her hip, cocking her head to

the side and letting her eyes sweep up and down my body. "Now who's wearing too many clothes?"

She had my jeans unbuttoned in a flash. The feel of her cool palm curling around my hard length had me letting out a raw groan. The next few moments were a blur as she freed me of my clothes. Her bra and panties joined the pile on the floor, but I wanted her to keep her sunshine socks on, an incongruous dash of whimsy.

Just when I thought I had control of the situation, she pushed me back, and my shoulders collided with the cool stainless steel surface of the refrigerator. She strung kisses over my chest as she teased my already aching cock to the point of pain with her hands. My fingers were laced in her hair when I felt the swirl of her tongue around the tip of my cock as she swiped a drop of pre-cum rolling out. Her naughty eyes caught mine when she sucked me in deeply. My free palm slapped against the refrigerator, and I gave myself over to her sucking, teasing touch. She drove me closer and closer to the edge.

She almost made me lose it, but I needed to be inside her. I clung to that need when I grabbed on to the frayed thread of my control. "Nora," I bit out on a ragged breath.

She leaned back, and I looked down to see her lips pink and damp. A rough growl escaped, and my cock pulsed with the need for release. Fortunately, I had wisely already pulled out a condom while we were getting my jeans off, and I snatched it off the counter, rolling it on in record time before lifting her again and walking from the fridge to the counter a few feet away.

Sliding her hips on the counter, I reached between her legs, finding her dripping wet from the juices of her arousal. "Mmm, I love it when you're like this."

I teased into her core with two fingers. "Always like this with you," she gasped.

"I know," I murmured as I brought her body flush against mine, her skin damp and warm everywhere we touched. "That's why we're right together." I notched my cock in the entrance of her body and filled her in one quick surge.

She cried out, arching into me, her pussy clenching around me. I was hanging onto my control with my fingertips, but I managed.

Chapter Sixteen

NORA

That's why we're right together.

Gabriel's gruff words sent a shiver coursing through my entire body right before he filled me. My body was chasing that sweet relief as he reached between us, teasing over my swollen and slippery clit. My orgasm was racing toward me, its force unstoppable.

"I know," I gasped as he drew back and filled me again, the sensation delicious and drugging.

"Come for me." His next words were the last push. "I love you."

My orgasm hit me in flying sparks, the pleasure piercing and sending my entire body into rough tremors as I gulped in air. He plunged into me once more, and I felt his cock pulse when he shuddered against me. My head fell to his shoulder, and he held me in his strong embrace as I sat there on the counter with my legs dangling around his hips.

This wasn't the first time my counter had seen some action with us. We had already christened every surface in my small house.

When he brushed my hair away from my eyes, I felt unsteady. My heart felt turned over in my chest, vulnerable and exposed. I swallowed, trying to catch my breath amidst the emotion spinning in the aftermath of my orgasm.

For the second time, Gabriel asked if I was going to send him home. For the second time, I didn't.

We fell asleep in my bed with his arm curled around my shoulders and my head tucked into the curve of his neck. I loved sleeping beside him. Because I felt safe. Safety and security were the two things I craved most in life.

Gabriel was strong and his touch sure. When we were asleep, I could pretend my baggage wasn't always in the way, bumping around and kicking people out of my life.

When I woke the following morning, it was still dark. Opening my eyes, I stared out the window beside my bed. The early glimmers of dawn winked, with the darkness a smudgy, charcoal gray and a few stars still visible in the sky. A thin glimmer of light shone above the mountain range in the trees as the first rays of the sun stretched up to the horizon.

I'd slept straight through the night, a rarity for me. That was a holdover from my childhood. My childhood had mostly been our mother and us. Flynn had been the most stable force in my life, if only because things were quieter when he was around.

In the night, if my stepfather was around, my parents argued. He wasn't violent; he was just an asshole. My mother always wanted more from him. She would go into the bathroom and lock the door and cry. He would go into the living room and watch television.

I would lay in my small bed, a familiar cold knot

forming in my stomach as I worried about how to make it all better for everyone. I craved my father's love and attention, yet I knew, even when I was really young, that I would never get it. It didn't change that little emotional lurch every time he appeared, and the uncertainty that followed because we were just waiting for when he would leave again.

My father didn't always leave for a woman. He simply wasn't built for commitment, or that was what he said to my mom time and again. I once heard him tell her he'd never planned to have children either. Apparently, he wasn't a fan of birth control, at least not with her. To this day, I wondered if we had other half siblings floating out in the world, unknown to us.

When Gabriel slept with me, I slept through the night, and I forgot all of that uncertainty. Oh, how I loved it. I savored it. It was like wrapping cold hands around a warm mug, the sensation of warmth comforting as it radiated everywhere.

This morning, Gabriel was curled up behind me, spooning me in his embrace. His knees were hooked into the bend of mine, and his palm was splayed over my belly. I wiggled my bottom back just a smidge and discovered the hard length of his arousal. He was almost always aroused in the morning. He swore it was just the way he was.

I felt it the second he came awake, a little vibration of awareness skating through his body. His palm tensed slightly on my belly before he relaxed it and moved it upward in a soothing stroke to cup one of my breasts. My nipples perked up, eager for his knowing touch when he lightly teased one with his fingers. His hand shifted, smoothing up over my shoulder before he brushed my hair away from my neck. Then I felt a light, barely-there kiss right where my shoulder met my neck. A sweet, hot shock reverberated through my entire body as all of my cells fired to life.

I was so ridiculously turned on by this man. He turned me into a needy, needy girl.

"I have a confession," he murmured, the motion of his lips on my skin sending jolts of sensation through me.

"I'm not your priest," I teased, letting out a little gasp when his hand moved down again and teased my other nipple.

"That's okay. I just wanted to tell you the truth."

His hands were still teasing me, mapping my body, and it was hard to focus. I tried to clear the haze and pay attention.

"About what?"

"I don't always wake up hard."

He flexed his hips, and I felt the presence of his arousal nestling between the cheeks of my bottom— hard and hot.

"You don't?" I gasped again when his teeth grazed my neck.

His hand moved down over the curve of my belly and dipped into the core of me. I was wet. It was entirely Gabriel's fault.

"Only with you," he murmured. "Only with you, Nora."

He rolled away from me, and I let out a protesting whimper, instantly missing him. But then I heard him reaching into the drawer beside my bed and the crinkle of a condom wrapper. In a second, he was rolling back toward me as I felt him smoothing it on. He lifted one of my thighs and sank smoothly inside me.

We made sleepy love as dawn broke. A ray of sun

crested on the horizon just as he sent me flying and shuddered against me with his own release.

I loved it. I loved waking up with him like this, and I loved that he told me he was only like this with me.

We showered and had coffee. And it was all so very good and so much of what I wanted.

Yet I struggled to hold on to faith in him, in me, in us. Well-worn paths of doubt blazed to life after he left. Because this was how good it felt before. How could I trust it?

Annoyed with myself, I spun around and grabbed my laptop, stuffing it into my backpack before I hustled up to the resort. Gabriel was headed out for some flights today, and I had some resort business to take care of. I handled all the scheduling and booking for flights as well as the resort. Daphne helped me with some of that, but the kitchen was her domain.

I told myself not to think too hard about Gabriel. I told myself all those silly things they recommended in self-help books. *Believe in yourself. Hope for the best. Just let life unfold.* Fuck.

I hated sayings like that because they annoyed the hell out of me.

I felt good this morning, though, good in a way I hadn't in a long time. I thought maybe, just maybe, I could believe Gabriel loved me.

There was a pretty big "maybe" to that, though.

Chapter Seventeen

NORA

"We're going to be late," Cat announced from where she sat beside me in the truck.

"I'm going as fast as this little truck will go," I countered, glancing sideways with a quick shrug.

"I don't want to interrupt Gemma's class after it started. It's not respectful."

I smiled. "I'm sure she'll appreciate that. We've got five minutes. We should make it in the nick of time."

We did, by a hair. Both Cat and I were nearly breathless as we unrolled our yoga mats and took our positions at the back of the classroom.

Gemma cast us a quick smile as she made her way around the room, leading the class and gracefully adjusting postures.

By the time we were lying down on the floor at the end of the class, I felt good. This was one of Gemma's faster-paced classes, and Cat and I loved coming to this one. Aside from the bonus of yoga, it was a nice way to spend time with my little sister. We had our own push and pull relationship. Over the past year, we had settled into a closer, less argumentative dynamic.

With Daphne here and such an integral part of Cat's life as her soon-to-be stepmother, because Flynn was basically her de facto father, it had eased the tensions between Cat and Flynn, as well as Cat and me. Somehow, Grant and Cat had floated along a little more comfortably over the years. Things had been hard after our mom died. Grant was just old enough not to argue as much with Cat but also not thrust into the role of functioning as her father the way Flynn had been.

I took several deep breaths, feeling the lingering twinges of tension ease in my body. A few moments later, people started getting up and putting their things away. Cat and I both changed out of our yoga leggings and tank tops into "town clothes," as Cat liked to call them.

We were headed over to Red Truck Coffee to talk with Cammi about planning her wedding. Her friends were helping her, but she wanted our feedback on how to make it special for Elias.

Gemma was waiting by the door as we approached. "Thanks for coming," she said with a warm smile.

"We love it. Sorry we were late," Cat said.

Gemma's brow furrowed. "I didn't think you were late."

"Cat thought we'd be late and didn't want to be disrespectful by coming in after you started," I explained.

Gemma grinned. "It would've been fine if you had actually been late. Life happens." She shrugged lightly. "I'll see you ladies at class at the resort next week. Diego and I are going to stay for dinner."

"You better," Cat said, shifting from her apologetic attitude about being late to apparently affronted at the thought that Gemma and Diego might even consider not staying for dinner.

Gemma curled her arm around Cat's shoulders and gave her a quick squeeze." I love having dinner with you."

"I hope so. Diego's my unofficial uncle, so now that you're with him, you're sort of becoming like my aunt," Cat said so earnestly that Gemma placed her hand over her heart.

"That's so sweet. I know he means a lot to you, and he considers all of you family. I feel lucky to be a part of it. Where are you ladies headed next?"

"Wedding planning with Cammi. Did you hear she's pregnant?"

"I did. Elias is going to be a family man. Diego is waiting for him to freak out. Not because he thinks Elias doesn't want kids, but because Diego thinks Elias is a worrier," Gemma replied with a wry smile.

My heart pinched a little. Elias was a reserved guy and hid it well, but he *was* a worrier, and he always liked to make sure everything was taken care of. Kids were messy and would definitely challenge that part of him.

I chuckled softly. "It should be fun to watch." A few students for the next class started entering the studio. "We'll see you at the resort. Thanks again," I called as we moved along.

A few minutes later, I aimed the truck toward Cammi's coffee truck.

"I can't believe Elias is going to have a baby," I said as I drove.

"Twins! He's having twins," Cat said, her eyes shining when she looked toward me.

I grinned. "I know."

"Do you think he'll let me babysit?"

"I'm sure he will."

A few minutes later, we pulled up in front of Red Truck Coffee. Cammi owned this place as well as Misty Mountain Café, which she'd taken over about six months ago. Red Truck Coffee was a Diamond Creek institution. It was an aptly named coffee shop housed in an old red baker's truck and had been around for years. Cammi kept it open from spring until the snow flew. Situated at the corner of the road that led to Otter Cove Harbor, it was the heartbeat of the small town in the summer when it was crowded with fishermen and tourists.

"Do you think we'll get some coffee?" Cat asked as we climbed out of the truck.

A chilly gust of wind blew off the harbor, the air crisp with a salty hint. "I would imagine so. Cammi is always generous with her coffee. At least we can insist on paying here."

We jogged across the gravel parking lot and knocked on the back door to the truck. Cammi had said she wanted us to meet her here because Misty Mountain Café was still open, but she'd closed the coffee truck earlier.

The door swung open, and Cammi smiled at us. It was no wonder Elias had fallen for her. She had an undeniable sweetness to her, so it made sense she would be the one to soften his guard. Her blue eyes twinkled as she gestured through the narrow doorway. "Come in."

I looked around the inside of the small space, commenting, "Even though I've been here hundreds of times, I've never been inside. It's tiny, but it doesn't feel crowded."

Cammi lifted her hands, tightening a ponytail holding up her honey-brown hair. "I did my best to make it spacious. When it's busy, there are two of us in here, and we need to be able to move."

The counter where she served customers was closed with the serving window folded down. She had shelving on the sides and above. She pointed toward a cluster of stools.

"Coffee?" she asked, gesturing for us to take a seat.

"Of course, but we're paying," I insisted.

Cammi pursed her lips and rolled her eyes. "No, you're not."

"Yes, we are," Cat chimed in.

Cammi laughed. "I've already shut down my laptop where I can ring you up. If you insist on giving me money, put it in the tip jar." She pointed at a Mason jar painted brightly with sunflowers. "The staff tomorrow morning will be thrilled."

While I stuffed a ten-dollar tip in the jar, she got to work making coffees for us. She made some tea for herself before she sat down, hooking her feet over the rungs on the stool. With a smile, she asked, "Okay, how do I make the wedding fun for Elias?"

Cat cast me a worried look before her eyes bounced to Cammi. "I don't know. Elias isn't really a party guy."

"I'm so excited for you two," I said, the backs of my eyes stinging with tears.

Elias was like another brother to me and Cat, one of Flynn's closest friends. He'd been a steady presence at the resort for over five years. While we were all thrilled for him and Cammi, we missed seeing him every day at the resort. We still saw him plenty because he worked at the resort flying planes, but it wasn't the same.

Cammi's cheeks flushed, and her eyes shifted down. Following her gaze, I finally noticed a ring.

"Oh, my God! He got you a ring?" I slapped my palm over my chest. "I already knew he loved you, but this is huge. Shopping for anything totally isn't his thing."

Cammi's smile was bashful when she looked up again.

Cat demanded, "Let us see."

Cammi uncurled her hand from the mug and held it out for us to see. It was a simple band with a sapphire.

"It's beautiful," Cat breathed.

"It really is," I said, my heart filled with joy for her and for them.

Cammi blinked when she looked up at us, and I thought she might be trying not to cry. "He picked it out himself and surprised me last week." Her voice was filled with wonderment as if she couldn't believe what had happened.

"Elias has had a thing for you for years. I knew one day he would get over himself. I didn't realize you two would reach the wedding and family stage this fast, though," I teased.

Cammi's cheeks went pink again. "I didn't either. I know he loves me. It's just when we first got together he didn't strike me as the kind of guy to settle down."

"He *is* that kind of guy. He just had to find you. He's one of the most loyal people I know," Cat offered, looking back and forth between Cammi and me.

"Oh, I know he is," Cammi said with a soft smile. She cleared her throat and took a swallow of her tea before continuing. "It means a lot to me that you two are willing to help me plan a little. I don't want anything elaborate. I thought maybe we could make the food whatever he wants. If you have any other ideas, I'd love that. I didn't want this to be something that was just planned by my friends. I consider you all my friends as well."

"It's only been since you and Elias started up that we've been more in your circle. You and I knew each other for years. It's just you were a few years ahead of me in high school. That's when everything is so defined," I commented.

"I know, it's so funny how it's like that," Cammi returned.

"Do you mean my world will be different when I'm done with high school?" Cat asked hopefully.

"Absolutely," Cammi said firmly. "It's such a weird time in your life, but you don't realize it until years later."

We settled in to look at what she had planned so far for their wedding and even did a conference call with Daphne for some menu ideas.

My mind kept slipping back to Cat's astute observation. That Elias was always the kind of guy to settle down, he just needed to find Cammy. I wondered if perhaps that was the case for Gabriel. I had a hard time envisioning myself as the kind of woman any man would fall for.

I kicked those thoughts to the curb and tried to stay focused. We had a wedding to help plan. I couldn't wait for it. Things were moving quickly for them now that Cammi was pregnant, and I loved that they had found each other.

I hefted a bag of gravel onto my shoulder and turned, taking a few steps to reach the small plane and place it in the back behind the seats. Turning, I repeated the task ten more times, to be specific.

I was delivering supplies to a community across the bay, along with dropping off some tourists in Seldovia, a picturesque town on the far shore of Kachemak Bay. It was one of the older towns in the area. However, it was off the road system, so the only way to reach it was by plane or boat. Despite its isolation, it was a tourist destination.

"Hello," a voice called from over by the parking area to the side of one of the plane hangars. Lifting my head, I saw two women approaching.

"You here for a flight with Walker Adventures?" I asked as they got closer.

"Yes." One woman nodded.

"You found the right place. Let me just grab a few things out of the office, and we'll be ready to roll. Do you have any bags with you?"

Grant came walking out of the hangar, casting an easy smile at the women. One of the women had long blond hair and big blue eyes, and the other was a brunette with dark eyes. Once upon a time, I would've happily spent hours flirting with both of them.

These days, I had zero interest in any woman other than Nora. I couldn't even summon any interest if I tried.

Grant, on the other hand, stopped beside them and flashed a smile. "I can get those bags if you need some help," he offered.

"That would be great," the dark-haired woman replied. "Follow me."

He walked with her over to their rental car while the blonde waited beside the plane hangar. "Can I help you with anything?" she asked.

"Nope. Just grabbing my bag." I snagged my backpack out of the office and slung it over my shoulder.

"By the way, I'm Gabriel," I said, stopping beside her again. "I'll be your pilot today."

She walked with me as I continued toward the plane. "I'm Lauren," she replied. "Alaska is amazing. How long is the flight today?"

"About thirty minutes, give or take."

"That's it?" Her eyes widened in surprise.

"All we have to do is fly across Kachemak Bay. It's not too far as the crow flies," I explained as I dropped my backpack into the front seat beside the pilot's seat.

Grant arrived with the other woman, who introduced herself as Samantha. He kept busy flirting with them while I took care of pre-flight checks. I considered offering this trip to him, but I knew he had an overnight trip booked. I wanted to be back at the resort tonight in the hopes that I could have another night with Nora.

After the women were situated in the plane, I made sure the compartment underneath was locked up and then paused with Grant outside. "How long will you be gone?" I asked.

"Three nights. You want to trade with me?" he returned with a quick grin.

I chuckled. "Nah, man. This is just a drop-off. They'll be back in town after this weekend, and then you can flirt to your heart's content."

"You just want to be back tonight because of Nora," he countered.

Ever since it had become public knowledge that I was trying to convince Nora I was worth it, Grant occasionally teased me. He was her brother, so I tried to tread lightly.

"Maybe so." I nudged him with my elbow. "Which is why I don't want to be gone for three nights."

He rolled his eyes. "All right, all right. See you when I get back. I'll be up in the air twenty minutes after you. Fly safe," he called as he backed away and turned to jog into the plane hangar.

Within a half hour, I was lowering the plane in the sky, taking in the mountains on the far side of the bay. The early autumn colors were pretty along the lower flanks of the mountains with yellow and gold leaves fluttering in the light breeze.

A few minutes later, I'd helped the passengers off the plane and started getting their bags out. When I heard the distinct sound of another two-seater plane engine, I glanced in the sky and recognized Nora's plane immediately.

It wasn't unusual for more than one of us from Walker Adventures to be passing through the same area. Until winter was here in full force, the tourist schedule kept us busy. Even after the snow flew, daily planes transported residents and carted supplies and mail to the various small communities scattered across Alaska. Walker Adventures was only one of a number of small flight businesses all over Alaska. To those who weren't familiar with the way Alaska functioned, it might seem improbable to have this many flights. But with so much of the state off the road system, planes were how people stayed connected. In some areas farther north, some hubs served fifty or more small communities. They were literally called air taxis.

Samantha glanced up in the air. "Wow, it's really busy here."

"Always," I replied as I handed her one of the bags.

Nora expertly landed, far clear of where we were waiting near one of the plane hangars.

"Do you all have a ride to town?" I asked, glancing at the women.

Right then, an SUV pulled in nearby. A woman got out, her dark hair streaked with gray and twisted into a braid, which swung as she jogged toward us. "Hey there!" she called.

I recognized Dana immediately. "Hey, Dana." I lifted my hand in a wave. Glancing at my two passengers, I added, "I'm guessing this is your ride."

Nora had parked her plane and climbed out. She was walking toward us. Even though this was absolutely not the place for my body to react to her, it was a given that it would. My cells sparked and fired, a familiar hum of anticipation sliding through me.

Lauren smiled up at me. "I don't suppose you all have any room at your resort next week?" Her question was innocent, but her tone was coquettish and her smile flirtatious.

Nora stopped beside us, greeting Dana first. I kept

my gaze neutral when I looked down at Lauren. "It's doubtful. We're usually booked well in advance. Nora would know that." I glanced at her, nudging my chin in her direction.

Lauren followed my gaze. "I was just asking our pilot here if your resort had any bookings available. It sounds like an amazing place."

Nora gave her a bland smile. "Unfortunately, no. We're usually booked out for the year by May."

"Well, that's too bad," Lauren replied. She gave me another dimpled smile, this time reaching over and squeezing me lightly on the elbow. "Maybe we'll see you around town when we're back from this part of our trip."

Dana caught my eye and chuckled. "You got any mail for us?" she asked.

"I think so." I strode back to my plane, opening the back compartment and scanning the mail bins. When my eyes landed on one labeled *Dana*, I reached for it. Like so many people in Alaska, Dana juggled multiple part-time jobs. She ran a bed & breakfast, along with managing the small post office here.

"Here you go." I handed the mail bin over to her. "Always good to see you. Catch you later, okay?"

With a wave, Dana departed with my two passengers, leaving Nora and me alone. "You must be picking up," I commented.

Nora nodded. Her shoulders were tight, and I watched as her eyes flicked over to the two women who were now climbing into Dana's vehicle.

"Yep," she replied when her eyes met mine again. She glanced at her watch. "Where are you headed next?"

"Don't you know?" I countered.

Her lips pressed in a line. I could tell she was thinking before she replied, "Oh, that's right. You've got to unload all that gravel first. Have fun with that."

I chuckled. I couldn't resist stepping closer and catching her hand in mine to reel her to me.

"Gabriel," she whispered.

"What?" I palmed her cheek, letting my thumb trace along her bottom lip.

Her eyes stayed locked on mine, and a wash of pink crested on her cheeks. "Um, we're in public."

"So, what? We're not a secret anymore, darling."

I let my hand slide into her silky brown curls before dipping my head and brushing my lips over hers. A sizzle of electricity passed between us, and I couldn't help the groan in my throat as I fit my mouth over hers, giving her a hungry kiss.

By the time we broke apart, my heartbeat was thundering through my body, and my breath was ragged. I couldn't let go just yet. I loved the feel of her body imprinted against mine, her curves soft, a contrast to my sharp edges.

The sound of a throat clearing audibly reached us. I glanced to the side to see an elderly man approaching.

"I always do love to see a young couple in love," Tom commented conversationally as he smiled at us.

Nora's cheeks flushed even pinker, and she stepped back, reaching up to tidy her hair from where I'd rumpled it. "Hey, Tom," she said.

"Always good to see you, Tom," I commented. "I have ten bags of gravel to unload."

Tom chuckled. "You'd better get started on that." He looked back toward Nora. "Gabriel's a good man. He hides it well, though."

Nora twisted her lips. "I know."

I wanted to kiss her again, but I didn't think she would go for it. We chatted about the weather, but I had to stay on schedule. With a wave, I returned to my plane and started unloading the bags of gravel.

Chapter Nineteen

NORA

It was nothing, nothing at all, I told myself for the perhaps twentieth time.

My brain was annoying the hell out of me, as it was wont to do when my insecurities started raging at me.

With auburn hair paired with flashing green eyes and that body, that freaking body—strong and rugged with all muscled planes—it was nothing to see a woman flirting with Gabriel. When he'd pulled me close for a kiss, by the time he drew back, my panties were damp, and I could feel the slick arousal between my thighs. My tight nipples were like my body's weathervane. However, they were tuned solely to the weather created by Gabriel in my vicinity.

Seeing that woman flirt with Gabriel reminded me of all the reasons he said he wasn't fit for commitment. His exact words had been, "I'm not a good bet. You know that, Nora."

I *did* know that. Until that fateful night when we finally gave in to the sparks flying between us, I'd known Gabriel to be a man who took the concept of casual quite literally. To my knowledge, he'd never spent more than one night with any woman. That detail had been what persuaded me it was safe to tell him I thought we had something. By that point in our relationship, or whatever it was, he'd spent far more than just one night with me. Our not-so-secret friends-with-benefits arrangement had been carrying on for over a year.

Then he'd gone and reminded me of all the reasons he couldn't be counted on. And now, he wanted me to believe he loved me.

I shook those thoughts loose, kicking them away. I had a packed flight schedule this afternoon. Tom was busy helping Gabriel unload the gravel he'd delivered. While they did that, I took care of loading a few parcels for the mail run back to Diamond Creek.

"See you tonight." Gabriel's voice came low by my ear, and a shiver chased down my spine as I turned.

"Of course. I think you'll be back before me," I replied, trying and utterly failing to play it cool. My cheeks were hot, and I was flustered.

"You'll be at dinner, though?" he prompted.

I felt a twinge of pettiness followed immediately by a more powerful pinch of guilt when I saw the uncertainty flicker in his eyes. I'd avoided him so thoroughly for months. Now that I wasn't, I didn't like admitting that a tiny part of me enjoyed the fact he wasn't sure of me.

"I will."

"Nora!" Tom called. "My appointment's in forty-five minutes."

Gabriel's lips kicked into a smile when he peered over my shoulder. "She's coming," he called in return.

He startled me again by bending low and palming my cheek as he gave me a quick and fierce kiss. The sweet shock of his lips meeting mine sent sparks scattering through me. When he lifted his head, I heard Tom's wry chuckle from behind us. "No wonder you're taking so long."

My cheeks burned hot as I turned away. Gabriel caught my hand and gave it a quick squeeze. "Tonight then." His words felt like a promise. I knew he could keep that promise. I just didn't know about the rest.

————

Tom was quiet as I lifted the plane into the air. A light gust of wind caught under one wing, and I leveled the plane in response. I'd known Tom since I'd been flying. He was a regular passenger with us.

This route, from Diamond Creek across the bay where we puddle-jumped from one community to the next, gave me plenty of experience with landing in dicey conditions. Alaska was famed for its bush pilots and the risks we took.

I loved my job. The concentration necessary to fly combined with the otherworldly views gave me a sense of peace I craved.

Tom slipped on the headset I'd handed him. I switched the channel to a private one so we could chat. "How've you been?" I began.

"As well as could be expected, but I'm having some trouble with my diabetes. That's why I'm going to the doctor today."

"Sorry to hear that. How's Darla?" I asked, referring to his wife, who was an absolute dear.

"She keeps me in line, that's for sure," he said, a low laugh rustling in his throat. "I've been wondering when you and your boy were going to prove me right."

I felt the heat creep up my cheeks, but I kept my eyes forward. "What do you mean?"

"I suspected you two had something going on for this past year or so."

"You did? It's not like I see you all that often," I teased.

"Nah, I've seen you two just enough to watch him. You didn't give it away, girl. It's always the man. We're stupid sometimes."

"You think so?"

"I know so. He's running from something though."

I wanted to ask Tom what he meant, but I suspected I already knew. I had only a sketch of Gabriel's childhood history, but it was scarred by his mother's abandonment. He didn't even like to talk about her.

"He loves you, though," Tom added, startling me so much I jumped in my seat and twisted to look at him.

His warm brown eyes regarded me, the laugh lines permanently etched into his weathered face. "I might not know much, but I know love when I see it. I knew that before I ever saw him kiss you."

My face was on fire by this point, and I forced myself to look away, mumbling, "I don't know how you can say that."

"Don't get in your own way. I'm an expert on that."

"You are?"

"Hell, yeah. Just ask Darla sometime. I loved that girl back in high school, and I almost screwed it all up because I thought we were too young. Thank God she took me back five years later."

I smiled over at him. "Guess you figured it out before it was too late then. How did you get in your own way? Age can't be the only excuse."

Tom shrugged. "Age *was* my excuse at the time, but my problem was my parents had a shitty marriage. Nothing complicated about it at all. I'm the product of them being too stupid to use birth control. Back then, people got married when that shit happened. My parents never really liked each other. It was just stupid. Not even awful. That old saying, death by a thousand cuts. I didn't have any grasp on what a good relationship looked like, so it kind of scared the shit out of me to have somebody really matter to me. You know?" Wordlessly, I nodded, and he continued. "Things do work out when they do. You get it when you get it. I suppose I had to break up with Darla to figure out nobody else compared. I'm just damn lucky she didn't fall for somebody else in the meantime. In your twenties, five years is a freaking lifetime."

I grinned. "I'm only twenty-five."

"You're a lot more mature than I was at that age. Although, I did have enough sense to snap Darla up by then."

I burst out laughing. "Always good to talk to you, Tom," I managed when I stopped laughing. Diamond Creek came into view. The pretty little town was situated at the base of the hillside with the mountains rising up behind it.

"You need a ride to your doctor's appointment?" I asked. My schedule was tight, but I would make it work if he needed a ride.

"No, ma'am. The doctor's office is sending me their version of a car service. It's not highfalutin like those city apps, whatever the hell they're called."

"It's not a car service. It's one of the receptionists driving down to the airport to pick you up because they have a soft spot for you," I teased.

"Hey, it's smart to be nice. That's something assholes never seem to figure out. That's not why I'm nice, but I never complain about the benefits," he offered with a sly grin.

After I delivered Tom where the as-promised receptionist from the local medical clinic was waiting, I dropped off the mail and picked up the next group of tourists. This was a flightseeing trip, my favorite kind. I flew a big, meandering loop through the sky, showing off the incredible views along the way and hoping we'd see some wildlife.

I got the opposite of Gabriel's pair of cute women. This was a pair of handsome, outdoorsy guys. They had *city* written all over them, primarily because they had expensive gear, and it was clean and barely worn.

One of the guys took a shine to me. He asked to sit up front and kept casting me what I interpreted to be flirtatious grins. I was terrible at flirting, just awful at it. I managed a few tight smiles in return until he picked up the headset and asked, "Will you meet us for drinks later?"

This kind of thing happened to the guys I worked with all the time, even the ones in committed relationships. This did *not* happen to me.

I knew my cheeks were bright red, and I didn't dare glance in the guy's direction. "I'm not so sure about that," I finally managed. "But thank you."

"You have no idea, do you?" he asked roughly two hours later after we had landed in Diamond Creek again, and they'd climbed out of the plane.

I stared up at him, treating it almost like an academic exercise. He had sandy blond hair and bright blue eyes. He gave off the vibe of one of those rich kids who had a ski pass in high school. Nothing like me. I had a ski pass here in Diamond Creek at the lodge. Not because I paid for it, but because we were friends with the owners. They gave all of our staff free ski passes because we offered to let them fly along on any trips for free as long as we were already going there and there was room.

I willed my body to feel a thing, something, maybe even a few butterflies. As I thought really hard, there was a tickle in my stomach, but when it growled, I realized it was because I was hungry.

He heard it and smiled. "I would buy you dinner, but you turned me down."

"Thank you, but I already have dinner plans. What do you mean, though? That I have no idea?" I couldn't help my curiosity.

"You're gorgeous. That's all. A woman who flies planes like a boss is a total badass and hot as far as I'm concerned." He winked as he turned away.

Wow. My ego could use a guy like him.

I didn't realize Gabriel was unloading my plane on the other side until I rounded it and found him there. "Oh, hey," I said.

He glanced up at me, and I could only describe the look he gave me as a glower. "Who the hell was that?" he muttered under his breath.

"That was Jonathon. Just a nice tourist."

Gabriel made some kind of growly sound.

"Are you jealous?" I asked incredulously.

Gabriel slung my bag over his shoulder as he narrowed his eyes. "Yes, I am. In fact, feel free to mock me."

Chapter Twenty

GABRIEL

Somehow, I ended up sitting at an angle across the table from Nora at dinner that night. Her hair was still damp from the shower she must've taken after returning to the resort. She was seated between two men, and I couldn't help but recall the guy who'd told her she was a badass and hot. She absolutely was.

An unfamiliar feeling of jealousy turned sour inside my gut. On any given week, at least two-thirds of our guests at the resort were men.

I couldn't recall if I'd ever even paid attention to how they looked. Surely, handsome guys had noticed Nora before. I'd never noticed anyone noticing her, not until this afternoon, and now again, tonight.

While I didn't bat for that team, I knew the guy sitting beside her tonight was handsome. His name was Nick something or other. I couldn't even hear what they were joking about because the table was full.

Cat happened to be sitting beside me and asked, "What's wrong?" She peered up at me with her slate-blue eyes, so similar to Flynn's and just as perceptive.

"Nothing," I replied, annoyed with the internal flare of defensiveness that rose inside.

Cat took a bite of her food, her gaze shifting away from me. Meanwhile, I couldn't resist glancing toward Nora again, only to see her laughing at something handsome Nick said.

Fuck this. It was hard enough to come to terms with my feelings for Nora. I did *not* appreciate, not one bit, the experience of jealousy.

"You're jealous." Cat's voice reached me, sounding amused.

I slid my eyes sideways, incredulous she'd commented on that.

Her eyes twinkled. "Just saying."

"I am not," I lied, injecting firmness into my tone. The whole thing was ridiculous.

Cat snorted a laugh. "Yeah, right. You just keep telling yourself that."

Fuck my life. I had a seventeen-year-old girl giving me shit about being jealous. By the time dinner was over, I was strung tight with annoyance and a sense of possessiveness. As fierce as my need for Nora ran, my feelings left me unsettled. I slipped out the back while she was in the kitchen helping Daphne, Cat, and Flynn clean up.

The autumn air was crisp. A light breeze gusted, carrying the spruce scent and causing the damp earthy leaves to fall to the ground. I walked into the trees behind the resort with quiet footfalls. I took a gulp of air, letting it out slowly as I paused to look through a clearing in the trees. It offered a view of a mountain ridge in the distance, the rising half-moon casting a silvery glow on the snowy peaks. The upper elevations had gotten more snow recently, a clear signal that winter was coming.

After another few breaths, I felt more like myself again. Turning, I kept walking, stuffing my hands in my pockets. I paused and glanced around when I heard a subtle scuffing. In a moment, my eyes found the source of the noise. A porcupine waddled through the trees, the tips of its quills gilded from the moonlight. I waited to move until it was a little farther away. Not because I was nervous about getting quilled, but because porcupines were shy creatures and mostly harmless unless they felt genuinely threatened. There was no need for me to frighten it. It was likely making its way to wherever it planned to sleep for the evening.

The trees opened up a few minutes later after I resumed my walk. I lifted my eyes to discover the staff house was dark. It appeared most were lingering back at the resort or heading into town to the bars. I'd lost all interest in going to town at night once I'd given in to my need for Nora. I was so accustomed to the fire that burned for her that it felt a part of me, woven into my veins and bones.

As much as I wanted to see her, my frustration with feeling possessive and jealous clashed with that desire. Just as I was about to move in the direction of the staff house, the sound of footsteps reached me.

Turning, I recognized Nora's silhouette through the trees instantly. I felt a tug in my heart, followed by that familiar jolt sizzling through me like fire.

She stopped at the edge of the trees, looking at me across the small clearing. After a beat, she approached me, stopping a few feet away. "I wondered where you went," she said.

For a second, the urge to make a flippant comment was right there, hovering in the edge of my consciousness. I didn't because *that* guy, the one who relied on dismissive comments, was the guy who had hurt Nora before. I felt thrown off my equilibrium, and I didn't know how to catch my balance again. I closed the distance between us with careful, deliberate strides.

When I paused in front of her, that sense of possessiveness flared. "I'm not sure where I was going either."

Her dark eyes widened. We were illuminated solely by the pearly glow of the moon.

I took a breath, letting it out slowly as I stepped closer and freed one of my hands from a pocket to slide it through the ends of her silky hair. "You make me a little crazy, you know?"

She shook her head incrementally. "I didn't know that. I don't think of myself as the kind of girl who makes anyone crazy."

A wry chuckle rustled in my throat. "No, you don't. That guy was right."

"What guy?"

"The guy who flew with you today."

She looked up at me, and I wasn't sure, but I sensed she flushed slightly. There wasn't enough light for me to know.

"Let me make this clear. You make me crazy, and I know it's not just me. You're beautiful, you're strong, and I want you. So, *so* much. Also, I was jealous twice today," I said with a wry twist to my words.

"Twice?" Her tone had a hitch of surprise to it.

"Yes, Nora, twice. First, when I heard that guy by the plane and then tonight at dinner. Nick likes you. I think his name is Nick."

She scoffed. "No, he doesn't. How would you even know that? And yes, his name is Nick."

"Because I'm a man, and he's a man. Trust me, I know he likes you."

She eyed me dubiously, pursing her lips as she

shook her head slightly and waved a hand dismissively. "Whatever. I'm not interested in Nick or that guy at the plane."

"No?" Finally, I asked the question that had been eating me up all afternoon and evening.

She shook her head firmly this time. "Just you. You make me a little crazy too." Her lashes swept down, and I slid my hand into her hair, cupping the back of her head and pulling her close. I felt her shiver.

"Let's go. You're cold," I murmured as I reluctantly eased back and reached for her hand.

She laced her fingers in mine, and we walked quickly through the trees to her place. Our breath misted in the air with every step along the way.

Moments later, the sound of the door slamming shut behind us as we stumbled into her house was another kick to the need already driving me fast. It was a pounding drumbeat through my body, the rhythm kicking faster and faster.

Unsettled as I was with the sense of possessiveness tangling inside my other emotions surrounding Nora, it created this feeling of intensity and exquisite intimacy. I felt as if I were standing on the edge of something immense and about to topple over. No one had *ever* mattered as much as her. No one had ever elicited feelings like that. I felt vulnerable, and my ability to protect myself from it was worn thin.

Nora was more important than my pride. With my heartbeat thundering in my ears, I kept her hand in mine, moving swiftly up the stairs and into her bedroom without pause after we kicked off our shoes and hung our jackets by the door.

"Gabriel—" she began as I set to unbuttoning her blouse.

"I need you," I bit out, my voice serrated on the edges.

"Oh," she whispered. "I'm right here."

Our clothes came off in a rush, and then my palms were sliding up her thighs, pushing them apart, savoring the tattered sound of her breath as I trailed kisses along the sensitive skin. I moved up swiftly because I needed her mouth underneath mine.

When she sighed into our kiss, her tongue gliding against mine, a sense of relief washed through me. *This* was what had frightened me about us before. Everything felt so absolutely right with her.

Chapter Twenty-One

NORA

"I'm going to make love to you," he said, each word slow and deliberate.

My heart ricocheted wildly in my chest, and I tried to catch my breath.

I felt caught in a rushing current of sensation and desire. The calloused surface of Gabriel's palms sent sparks raining over my skin. His lips felt like hot drops of honey as he pressed them just inside my calf and then on my thigh. One palm was on my belly, his thumb moving in an idle path, sending heated pinwheels throughout my body.

I was near frantic by the time his fingers teased my folds. I was slippery wet, and I heard his low growl of satisfaction, the hum of it reverberating as he brought his mouth to me.

He made love to me with his mouth and his fingers and his tongue, sending me spiraling higher and higher, chasing after the sweet release I craved. By the time it broke over me, I was near incoherent in a sharp burst of exquisite relief.

Then he was rising above me, and I welcomed his

weight, savoring his musky scent and the firm press of his body against mine. He was always prepared, this man. I didn't even know when he'd gotten a condom on, but he had. In a fevered second, he was sliding inside me, the thick, delicious feel of him filling me. My voice was slurred when I murmured, "Gabriel."

"Right here, darling." His lips dusted along the side of my neck, sending hot shivers rippling through me as he drove into me in slow, steady surges.

I was restless underneath him, already chasing after more. I had no idea how long it lasted, but he brought me to another body-shaking release just before he found his own. He collapsed on me before rolling swiftly to the side and bringing me with him. We lay there gasping for air together. The sound of my heartbeat echoed in my ears, and my breath came in tattered gulps.

We'd been intimate many times, but I'd never felt like this. It felt as if something had fallen and given way between us. Simply lying there in the aftermath with him holding me, it felt as if my emotions were pressing against my skin.

This would usually make me anxious, because Gabriel always held himself at bay a little. Yet, when I lifted my drowsy eyelids, I found his gaze waiting. The layer of distance was gone, and he looked almost boyish.

The lamp in the corner of my bedroom, which I had no idea had even been turned on in the midst of our rush, cast a soft glow over him, gilding his auburn hair with flickers of gold.

"Well," he murmured.

I laid still, letting my fingers draw circles on his chest and wondering if I could let myself have faith in us.

Chapter Twenty-Two

GABRIEL

"Okay, what's the schedule?" Tucker asked. His voice was muffled because he was leaning into the back of one of the planes.

I glanced at the screen on my phone, reviewing an email Nora had just sent with our flight schedules. "You're doing the mail run, I have some supplies to deliver, and then we both have a few sightseeing trips this afternoon."

Tucker straightened, closing the door to the back of the plane and leaning against it as he crossed his arms. "Well, it sounds like we're gonna have the same kind of day." His bright blue eyes coasted over me. "You're looking cheerful this morning. Have a good night with Nora?"

I grinned. "Everything with Nora is good." I didn't speak it aloud, but it was such a profound relief we weren't trying to hide *us* anymore.

Tucker flashed me a quick smile before his gaze sobered. "Flynn's still worried you're gonna break her heart again."

Stuffing my hands in my pockets, I sighed as I

scuffed the toe of my boot over the pavement. "I know he is. I won't though."

He nodded. "Good. I think you're good for each other." He pushed away from the plane before curling his palm over my shoulder and giving it a squeeze. "I'll see you later. Are we landing around the same time?"

I glanced at my phone again and lifted my eyes to his again. "Yep."

"Want to grab some burgers and beer at the brewery?"

I checked my hesitation and nodded. "Sounds good." I always wanted to get back to Nora as soon as I could these days, but I also valued time with my friends.

Later that evening, I pocketed my keys and walked quickly across the parking lot toward Diamond Creek Brewery. This was a favorite place for locals as well as tourists. It was a busy brewery, and, in addition to beer, and they also offered wines, mead, and had recently begun producing a local mulled cider. Along with all of that, they had an excellent restaurant.

I pushed through the doorway into the restaurant. It was housed in a renovated plane hangar. Tucker had texted me that he'd snagged us a booth in the corner by the windows. My eyes scanned the area, and when my gaze landed on his, I lifted my hand in a wave as I threaded my way through the tables.

Tables filled the center of the space with booths lining the walls. In honor of its location as a former plane hangar, small model planes hung from the ceiling in whimsical decoration. The expansive space had rugs scattered on the floors to soften the noise.

I didn't think I'd ever been here at a time when it wasn't crowded, and tonight was no exception. I was relieved Tucker had landed a little earlier than me.

Otherwise, I didn't doubt we would be waiting for a table.

Sliding into the booth across from him, I smiled. "Thanks for beating me here. I'm freaking starving, and I can definitely use a beer."

Tucker grinned. "My timing was good. A group was just leaving when I got here. I've already ordered us two beers. I'm assuming the house draft will do for you?"

"You know me well," I teased.

"Any problems today?" he asked.

"Not a one. Every flight went smoothly. The wildlife cooperated for my scenic trips."

Tucker chuckled, leaning back in the booth and running a hand through his shaggy brown curls. "Same here. We saw a brown bear by the water. Near Halibut Cove, we saw some moose and even a few sea lions chilling out on the rocks."

"Sweet. We saw everything but the sea lions."

My phone rang, and I reached into my pocket to slide it out. Glancing at the screen, I saw my mother's name. "This is my mom. Mind if I take it real quick?"

He shook his head. "Of course not. I gotta run to the boys' room anyway."

He slipped out of the booth as I answered, "Hey, Mom. What's up?"

"Gabriel!" She opened every call with me like that, her tone sounding surprised.

Considering that I answered every call from her unless I was in the middle of something, it grated on me.

"How's it going?" I asked, preparing myself for the inevitable request for money.

"Oh, fine, fine," she chirped. "You?"

"Doing well. Busy, as usual." I was already annoyed

with this call, I wanted to hurry it long. "What can I do for you, Mom?"

"You know, Gabriel, I'm not always calling for something. Maybe I just wanted to say hello," she replied defensively.

I swallowed my sigh and leaned back in the booth, feeling weary. "I don't mind that you ask for things, Mom. I do mind the bullshit though."

She went quiet. I could picture her face, her lips tightening in a line, and her eyes flicking down. Life hadn't been kind to my mother, and that was the only reason I had any patience with the strange relationship we had. If I could even call it a relationship. Her family life growing up had been unstable, so she struggled with alcohol and stability.

Having two kids when she was young wasn't a great recipe for her to pull it together. Pressure only added to her general state of distress. She bounced in and out of our lives, gracing us with her presence whenever she needed somewhere to stay. Fortunately, my dad was solid as a rock. I made a mental note to give him a call. He wasn't much for chatting on the phone, but we were tight. My relationship with him was definitely more about quality rather than quantity.

My mother's sigh filtered through the phone line as I waited. "I'm sorry you view it that way. I do appreciate the money you sent me earlier. It turns out—"

My impatience got the best of me. "Just tell me how much you need."

"I need rent money again. A thousand dollars."

"I'll wire it over tomorrow morning. I thought you were about to buy a place," I said. I knew better than to make that last comment because my mom often had plans fall through. In her world, she could merely be thinking about buying a home or wishing she could for it to be considered a plan.

She was quiet for a second before replying, "It didn't work out."

"No problem. Like I said, I'll help."

This time, her sigh was one of relief as it came out in a rush. "Thank you, I really appreciate it. Have you talked to your sister recently?"

I bit back a groan. "No, Mom. You know she's not big on phone calls. We text pretty regularly. Next time I talk to her, I'll let her know you'd like to hear from her."

My relationship with my sister was similar to that with my dad, with a little more distance. Because the world was what it was, adolescence had been hard on her, and we'd grown apart. Independence was really important to her. She wasn't a fan of our mom. She carried more resentment than I did, which was saying something, so she rarely spoke with Mom.

"That would be great," my mother replied with a forced cheerfulness in her tone.

After I replied with, "Mmm," my mom fell silent.

I knew we were now at that point of the conversation where she was trying to figure out how to get off the call gracefully. Rather than wait her out, I pushed ahead. "All right. Well, do you need anything else?"

"I don't think so," she chirped, her bright tone scraping over my nerves.

"Take care, Mom." I hung up after she mumbled a goodbye.

Tucker returned at that moment, just as a waitress arrived with our beers. He sat down, and the waitress, a friendly, outdoorsy-looking type with her dark hair up in a ponytail, set our beers down in front of us. She pulled out a small computer tablet. "Okay, guys, are you ready to order some food?"

"I'll take a burger and fries. Medium rare, please," I said.

Tucker flashed a grin at me before he looked up at the waitress. "Same here, except make my burger well done."

"You've got it. If you need anything else, just wave when I'm nearby. Food should be out in about fifteen minutes."

She hurried off, and I lifted my pint glass to take a swallow of beer.

When I set it down, I collided with Tucker's curious gaze. "What's up?" he asked.

"Nothing new since you went to the restroom."

He arched a single brow. "You didn't look cranky before I went to the restroom, and now you do."

I took another swallow of beer. Setting the glass down, I traced my fingertip around the base. "You know my mom. She's always calling for money. It gets old, but I'd feel worse if I didn't help her out."

He nodded. He knew the situation with my mother and had even met her once. When we were in the Air Force together and on break, she'd stopped by.

"You don't have to give her money, you know."

I leaned my head back, resting it on the booth. "I know I don't, but whenever I don't, I feel guilty. I'd rather feel annoyed than guilty."

His mouth twisted in understanding, and he shrugged. "I get it. There's no good answer. How are things with Nora?"

"Pretty good. I think."

Tucker's eyes took on a glint. "Keep them good. Don't let this shit get in the way."

"What the hell do you mean by that?" I returned, defensiveness flaring inside.

"I mean, it doesn't take a rocket scientist to figure out why you've got problems with commitment, or used to. Your mom has been a flake in every important relationship in her life. It's no wonder it's hard for you to believe it can work out."

"Damn," I muttered. "I don't need to be psychoanalyzed by you, or anyone else for that matter. Things are good with Nora, and they're going to stay that way."

"Chill out. I wasn't trying to piss you off, just making an observation. My sister always says you have to understand your past to make things better in the future."

I opened my mouth to counter that, and he chuckled. "Dude, she's a therapist. She knows shit like that."

I rolled my shoulders and took another swallow of beer. "Fine. I'll work on understanding my past," I offered dryly.

Later that night, when I texted Nora to tell her I wanted to come by, she replied she wasn't feeling well and didn't want to give me her cold.

I wanted to argue the point, but she read my mind from a distance. *Getting sick is stupid.*

Chapter Twenty-Three

NORA

I got a nasty cold that lasted over a week. Preferring not to pass it on to guests who were traveling and ruin their vacation with a cold, we shuffled the schedule around so I didn't handle any flights. I mostly holed up in my place. Gabriel stopped by a few times, but it was impossible for him not to notice I was sick. He was sweet, though, and delivered some homemade chicken and dumpling soup, made especially for me by Daphne.

When I finally started to feel better, I ventured into town to run some errands one afternoon. I was making my way through the grocery store when I felt the hairs on the back of my neck rise and a pleasant shiver chase down my spine. The sound of Gabriel's voice the next aisle over set me off.

I felt good enough to speed up, bringing my cart around the end of the aisle and turning it into the one where he was. He was standing about halfway down, one hand hooked in his pocket as he spoke on the phone.

Just as I reached him, I heard him say, "No problem, Mom. I gotta go. I'm at the store."

He slipped his phone in his pocket just as he looked up and saw me approaching. When one corner of his mouth kicked up in a slow smile, my belly executed a quick flip, and butterflies tickled the inside. The rapid tap of my pulse sped when I stopped in front of him.

"Hey there," he murmured, his voice low and intimate. "Rumor has it you're flying tomorrow."

"Uh, yeah," I said slowly. "I texted you about the flight schedule this morning."

His eyes skated over my face. "I'm glad you feel better."

"Same here," I replied, stating the obvious. "How's your mom?"

The moment I asked that question, his entire demeanor shifted. His gaze shuttered, and he shrugged, feigning nonchalance. The tightness around his eyes and the set of his shoulders gave away his instant tension. "Fine." His tone was sharp, clearly putting an end to this topic of conversation.

Maybe it was because I'd been sick for a week, maybe it was because I missed him, or maybe it was because I picked the absolute worst time to start a conversation about something that mattered, but I snapped at him.

"You know, if we're really going to try to do this, we have to be able to talk about uncomfortable things. I understand what it's like to have a parent who's mostly absent."

Gabriel just stared at me, and when he shrugged again, that annoyed the hell out of me. "I'd prefer not to talk about it here," he finally said.

Feeling peevish, I shrugged. "Fine. I'll be at dinner at the resort tonight."

Somehow, we moved past that little stumbling block I'd unintentionally created. He finished shopping with me and even helped me load the groceries in the truck. Just before I climbed in, he kissed me, pressing his forehead to mine briefly. "Do I get to do more than bring you chicken soup tonight?"

I felt the curve of his smile against my lips. "Yes," I whispered.

———

Dinner at the resort was the usual controlled chaos. We were serving guests tonight, so it was far too busy to relax and hang out. I made my way back to my house early. While I did feel better, I was still tiring easily and was weary from running errands and then helping Daphne and Cat get everything ready for dinner.

Gabriel came over, and it was nice. Not because we had crazy hot sex, but rather because we relaxed in front of the television and just chilled out. I fell asleep curled up against him.

When I woke the following morning, the brief conversation about his mother in the grocery store felt like a grain of sand in my shoe. I had enough sense to know trying to chat about a potentially emotionally loaded topic in the grocery store wasn't a smart move. But I didn't want to leave it unspoken. If Gabriel loved me and if we were going to try to do this, we had to be able to talk. Love wasn't all rainbows and fun.

Maybe I'd never had a good serious relationship, not even close if I was being honest, but I knew making things work wasn't always easy. As I was prepping the coffee, I decided I would ask Gabriel about his mom again. He'd given me a sketch of her role in his life, or primarily lack thereof, but that was it.

I was sipping my coffee when he emerged from the bedroom after a shower. With his auburn hair darker when it was damp, his green eyes stood out in contrast. No matter the moment, all of my cells cheered at the sight of him.

"Good morning," I said when he stopped in front of me.

He dipped his head, murmuring against my lips, "Good morning." He gave me a lingering kiss before drawing back. "Thanks for making coffee."

He lifted the empty mug I'd set beside the coffee pot and filled it. "I toasted bagels too. You just need to heat the cream cheese. Daphne made a fresh batch yesterday afternoon, so I brought some home with me."

Not much later, we'd both polished off one of Daphne's delicious bagels with smoked salmon cream cheese. Living in Alaska and having the benefit of the natural bounty of fresh salmon could be decadent.

Looking across the table at Gabriel, I steeled myself and began, "I know my timing wasn't good yesterday, but how is your mom? You never talk about her."

His eyes tightened at the corners, and he pursed his lips before he took a quick sip of coffee. When he looked back over the table at me, he gave a dismissive shrug. "There's not much to say. She's fine. Why do you want to talk about her? It's not like you discuss your father that much."

His words felt barbed, but I held my ground. "My father's dead. If he were alive, I'd probably have more to say about him. You know everything there is to know. He was hardly around and cheated on my mom a lot. That about sums it up."

Gabriel's eyes searched mine. "My mom is fine. We're not close," he finally said.

I didn't know what it was about this topic, but it felt like it represented something important to us. "I know you're not close, but why are you so defensive when I ask?"

"I'm not defensive," he countered, his tone belying his words. It was sharp, pointed, and clearly annoyed.

"How do you know you love me?" I asked next because *that* was a smart thing to do. I didn't even know that question had been hovering in my thoughts, but now it was out there.

His eyes widened. "What the hell do you mean? Is this some kind of test? If I don't bare my soul to you about my mother, then I don't love you. What the fuck, Nora?"

Anxiety coiled tightly in my chest, and I felt hot and cold simultaneously. "It's not a test. But how *do* you know? If we can't even have a simple conversation about your mother, how are we going to handle things that aren't easy?"

Gabriel's eyes widened and then narrowed. "I don't know how to explain it. I just know I love you. I don't really understand what's happening right now," he muttered.

"You know what? I don't think you're ready. Or maybe I'm not ready." I stood abruptly from the table, an unsteady sensation racing through me as my stomach clenched with dread.

"What do you mean, Nora?" Gabriel stood with me, and we stared at each other across the table.

"I don't really know. I just know this doesn't feel right. We need a break." My words tumbled out.

"A break?"

Chapter Twenty-Four

GABRIEL

Nora's brown eyes were wide, and color flagged high on her cheeks. "Yes, a break. I was already stupid once with you. I don't want to be stupid again."

Panic churned in my gut. In the span of only minutes, Nora punched the biggest button I had—my mother. I fucking hated talking about my mother. Now, Nora wanted a break and wanted to know how I knew I loved her? I didn't even know how to answer that question.

Anger flashed cold and then hot inside me. "Fine. Fuck you. If you don't want to believe me and you don't want to give us a chance, then it's not worth it. I'm not going to grovel for you."

With anger driving me, I stalked out of her house. The cold frost on the ground crunched under my feet as I walked through the trees. I felt sick inside.

I loved Nora. She didn't even understand how much I loved her. I didn't know what to do with her frustration, but I didn't want to discuss my mom, who had never been there for me and likely never would.

I made my way back to the staff house and grabbed my bag, then headed out for my flights that day.

Chapter Twenty-Five

NORA

"Oh God, it's a little icy," Cat said.

"It is, but you've got it."

Cat glanced my way quickly, her eyes wide. "Maybe I should pull over, and you should drive."

I looked ahead at the perfectly level road. "No, I think you should drive. The speed limit is twenty-five here, and it's not that icy. You drove over a patch of it because of the shade back there."

Cat pressed her tongue into the corner of her mouth, something she did when she was stressed and thinking hard. Her hands were clenching the steering wheel.

"Are you sure?"

Although I knew she needed to learn to handle ice when she was driving, if Cat actually fessed up to being nervous, she was *really* nervous. My little sister was the most stubborn human being I'd ever encountered, and she hated, absolutely detested, admitting she was nervous.

"If you're not comfortable, just pull over. Up there at the grocery store would be good."

Cat did as I instructed. Once she was parked, she climbed out as if she were a scalded cat. She practically ran around to the other side of the truck. I hopped out, and we switched seats. I had to slide the driver's seat forward a little.

"You're taller than me," I said with a quick smile in her direction. "When did that happen?"

My sister's anxiety was already gone, and a wide smile stretched across her face. "I don't know. You didn't notice, yet you see me every day. I didn't even realize."

"I had to pull the seat up. Not far, but enough to know you're taller than me now."

I started driving again. We were on our way back from yoga class and the final planning meeting for Cammi's wedding, which was scheduled for this coming weekend.

"The thing with ice is to never slam on your brakes," I explained. "Always tap. You get better traction by slowing down instead of speeding up. If you feel yourself losing traction, just ease your foot off the gas pedal. That gives the tires a minute to catch. I think we should ask Flynn to do with you what he did with Grant and me."

"What's that?" Cat asked, her tone dripping with suspicion.

"He took us to an empty parking lot in the winter, and we drove around, practicing getting things under control after skidding. He even made us skid on purpose."

When I slid my eyes sideways, Cat looked horrified. Her mouth was open, and her eyes were wide. "That's insane," she said flatly.

"Not really," I said with a little shrug. "It's safe because no one else is around, and you can get the feel of losing control without worrying about everybody around you. That's how I learned to drive a stick shift."

"Huh?"

"Because when the road is slick, if you don't shift properly when the car stutters, you're likely to keep rolling, so it's easier to correct. Benefits of living in a cold place," I added with a chuckle.

"I still think that's insane."

"You might think it's fun. Grant did."

Cat snorted. "Of course, he did."

Cat's phone vibrated from where it sat on the dashboard in front of her. She reached for it, then glanced at the screen. When she lowered the phone, I commented, "You can answer it. I don't mind."

"I know." When she still didn't answer her phone, I cast my eyes sideways briefly and saw the pink blooming on her cheeks.

"Who is it?" I kept my tone light.

"It's Julian."

"Oh?"

Cat let out a put-upon sigh. "Fine. We might be dating."

"Um, I didn't even ask if you were dating." My lips twitched, but I resisted the urge to smile. Cat wouldn't appreciate that.

"I know, but you were about to."

"Well, I like Julian," I said quickly. "Doesn't he work for the Winters brothers in the summer?"

"Uh-huh."

"I thought you were already friends. Or am I confused?" I pressed.

The truth was, I was shameless when it came to Cat and dating. She had a sketchy experience with one guy who tried to pressure her, and then her last boyfriend cheated on her. She was already working up to be cynical about relationships, and I didn't want that to happen to her.

"Yeah, we're friends. Or maybe more." Cat sounded young and vulnerable. Even though she was only seventeen, she rarely sounded vulnerable. My heart pinched.

"I don't understand how to do the dating thing," she added.

I reached over and squeezed her hand quickly, where it rested on her thigh, before releasing it. "It might seem like other people know what they're doing, but they usually don't. Not at that age. Even when we get older, most of us are just stumbling around trying to figure things out."

"Like you and Gabriel?"

She caught me there. I'd walked right into that one.

I laughed softly, ignoring the stinging burn over my heart. "Point taken. Before you completely shut me out of this conversation, I want to say one thing. Just because some guys are assholes doesn't mean everyone is. It's worth trying again."

"You mean like Dad was an asshole?" Her tone was quiet and almost hesitant, so uncharacteristic of my little sister.

I whipped my gaze to hers as I came to a jerking stop at a stoplight before we turned onto the highway that would lead us home.

"What do you mean?" Somehow, I'd convinced myself that Cat hadn't been as affected by our father's unreliable presence in our lives—not to the extent that Flynn, Grant, and I had. She'd been so young when he died.

"I know you guys think I didn't notice, but of

course, I did. Mom was always crying. It was usually better when he wasn't around. First, Mom would be all mopey. Then she'd get over it and be more like herself. Until he would show up again and make her all kinds of promises. What a dumbass."

A horn honked behind me, and I looked ahead to see the light had changed to green. I turned onto the highway, keeping my gaze on the road. I carefully considered my words. "Dad couldn't be reliable. I'm sorry it affected you too. It doesn't change what I said, though."

"I know. I'm not scared to try again with someone. Not yet. I'm just a little nervous because Julian's my friend, and I don't want to screw that up."

"Smart move. Things can get complicated with friends."

"Since you brought it up again, can we talk about you and Gabriel?"

I bit the insides of my cheeks for a minute and sighed. "Fine. What do you want to talk about?"

"I think you're making a mistake. I thought so before," she said hurriedly.

"What are you talking about?" I was flabbergasted. I had not talked to anyone about my choice to break things off recently. That said, I knew undercurrents were rumbling. I felt them every time I was anywhere near Gabriel.

Cat's ponytail bounced as she bobbed her head up and down when I glanced her way again. "Yes. I don't think he knows how to be in a relationship. But neither do you," she added softly.

My eyes stung, and my throat felt thick. My little sister was getting all grown up and giving me advice about my love life, and I didn't know how to deal with it.

"Well, that's a fact. I don't know how to do relationships," I finally said. "We're figuring it out, I think."

Cat wasn't done with me yet. She pressed on. "I think he's kind of freaked out by how he feels about you. He's been awfully cranky since you broke up with him."

"How do you know I actually broke up with him?" I countered, promptly revealing that I, in fact, had been the one to break things off. Again.

"Because I do. He didn't say anything, if you're wondering. I asked Flynn and Daphne if Gabriel said anything, and she said he was heartbroken."

I groaned. "Oh, my God. I'm gossip at work."

Cat cast me a wry grin. "That's what you get for owning a business with your family. We don't have to keep talking about it. I'm sure you hate it about as much as I hate you giving me advice right now. I'm just saying don't ruin a good thing."

Chapter Twenty-Six

GABRIEL

I shifted my shoulders and ran my finger along the edge of my shirt collar. I wasn't accustomed to wearing a suit. Elias was getting married, and I was one of the groomsmen with Tucker, Flynn, and Diego. Elias wanted all of us to stand up with him. He insisted he wouldn't have met Cammi if it weren't for us because we were the reason he came to Alaska. I tried to slide out of it by pointing out that Flynn was the one who invited all of us to come work with him in Alaska.

Elias had scoffed and cuffed me lightly on the shoulder. "As soon as the ceremony is over, you can take off that suit and chill out in jeans and a T-shirt for the reception."

"Seriously?" Diego had prompted.

Elias grinned. "That was my agreement with Cammi. She wants the whole deal for the ceremony, but she said she doesn't care about what happens afterward."

Nonetheless, wearing a suit wasn't something I did often. I shifted my shoulders again, feeling stiff and uncomfortable. This day felt big, really big. In a weird way, Elias and I had bonded over never planning to get serious. We weren't assholes, and we weren't players. We had merely dedicated ourselves to being casual for years.

Elias was deeply content with Cammi, and I was so fucking happy for him. I was also still puzzling over the riddle of Nora breaking things off with me. I was trying to figure out why she was so upset. What did she expect me to say about my mother?

I felt a nudge on my shoulder. Diego's tone was low. "We're moving."

I took a quick step forward, and we lined up. We had a cold snap last week, and Cammi had worried it would ruin their outdoor ceremony. Autumn in Alaska was fickle. Some days were cold and some warmer. The weather gods and goddesses shined down upon them, and we had a beautiful, if slightly brisk, sunny day for their wedding on the property where Cammi had grown up. Elias had snapped it up when the owners decided to put it on the market.

It truly felt as if everything was falling into place for them. When I watched Cammi, stunning and radiant in her wedding dress, look into Elias's eyes as he easily made his vow to protect her forever, I listened and wondered if something was missing for me. I knew I loved Nora, but maybe I just wasn't cut out for love the way my friends were finding it.

I couldn't help but sneak glances at Nora. Hell, I'd been stealing glances of her for years now, tucking memories away. While she was speaking to me these days, everything between us felt stilted and polite, and I wanted to scream sometimes.

After the ceremony, I happened to be standing

nearby when Nora caught Cammi's bouquet of peonies. Some of the petals fell on the ground, surrounding her feet.

"What am I gonna do with these?" Nora mused, her tone annoyed as she eyed them in her hand.

Elias's sister laughed. "I guess you're gonna fall in love."

Nora's eyes lifted to hers, narrowing. "Fat chance of that. I don't believe in love."

Diego, who happened to be nearby, pressed his fist on his chest over his heart. "How can you say that? Love is a real thing. Do you believe in Elias and Cammi?"

Nora's hard stare shifted to him. "Of course, I believe in Elias and Cammi. Love just isn't for me. I don't think I have the right personality."

Diego rested his palm on her shoulder, giving it a light squeeze. "You'll know when it's right."

Nora glared at him.

Her words repeated in my mind. *I don't believe in love.*

My heart twisted because *I* believed in love, and I *had* to find a way to get her to believe we were worth it.

That night, I was lounging on the sofa in the house, flicking aimlessly through the TV channels. Grant was with me, and he finally said, "Dude, just keep it on the football game."

I slid my gaze sideways. "Fine."

He gave me a long look. "You're cranky."

Harley happened to be coming down the stairs at that moment. "You are. What gives?"

She plopped down on the couch on the sectional across from me, hooking her toes under the edge of the coffee table and sliding it a little closer to her before propping her feet on it and crossing her ankles.

"Nothing," I muttered before tossing the remote to Grant.

Harley's brows lifted, and she pursed her lips as she gave me a considering look. "It's not nothing. Is it the wedding?"

"No. I'm very happy for Elias and Cammi."

She rolled her eyes at that. "I know that. I was thinking maybe the wedding reminded you that you're being an idiot about Nora."

I narrowed my eyes. "She's the one who broke it off with me. Again," I replied defensively.

"Maybe so, but maybe you could try to fight a little harder," Harley offered pointedly.

I looked toward Grant, who simply shrugged. "I'm not the expert on romance, but Harley's got a point."

I leaned my head back on the couch, letting out a groan. "Fuck my life. I don't know what to do." I lifted my head, being more honest than I wanted to be, but I was desperate. "Maybe I'm not cut out for love."

Harley snorted. "Well, if you don't think you are, that's a self-fulfilling prophecy. For what it's worth, Nora is being an idiot too. You're both stubborn."

I gave her a long look. "You're stubborn too."

Harley threw her hands up in the air and let them fall with a thwack onto the couch. "It doesn't matter if I'm stubborn. I'm not going to argue that I'm not. I can't solve this riddle for you two. It's obvious you love each other, and it's obvious you want to be together. All I'm saying is if you give up, well, then you're giving up."

"Thanks for stating the obvious," I deadpanned.

Grant divided his gaze between us before offering, "Obvious or not, either you try or you don't."

"She's your sister," I said, annoyed with my irritation about the situation. "Maybe you can tell me what to do."

Grant was quiet for a few beats as he leaned back on the couch. "You have to understand, Nora doesn't trust easily. I think you already knew that, but be patient. She's expecting you to give up."

"Has she said that?"

"No. It's just the way she is. You know the outlines of our dad, but he was a total flake. Never really around and always breaking our mom's heart. Nora is stubborn, and as Harley pointed out, so are you. If you really want Nora and you really love her, then you have to fight for her."

———

The following day, I headed out to Otter Cove Harbor with Nathan Winters on a silver salmon fishing jaunt. When I told Daphne he'd texted me about the open spot on the boat, she was delighted and already planning what she might cook with the fresh salmon.

The gravel crunched under my feet as I walked across the parking area. I paused at the top of the docks, looking beyond the harbor into Kachemak Bay. I knew for a fact there were postcards of this view because I'd sent one to my sister just last summer.

It wasn't long before we were headed out into the bay. After Elias's wedding and all the fucking feelings it'd brought up for me, I was relieved to be out on the water. There was a light breeze today, and the crisp, salt-tinged air was refreshing. The group caught their limit pretty quickly, and we were on our way back when we heard a mayday call over the radio. Nathan glanced at me. "We're about fifteen minutes from those coordinates."

"Let's head over that way. The Coast Guard will come too, right?"

"Oh, yeah," he replied quickly. "They'll send out a rescue team right away. It's just we're closer than they are."

We hightailed it over there. It was hard to tell what happened, but the boat was well on its way to sinking. A group of passengers huddled in a lifeboat, and Nathan cut his speed down to no-wake. We reached the group and quickly got everyone on board.

"What happened?" I asked one of the guys once he was off the lifeboat and onto ours.

He looked distressed. "I'm not sure," he said, his teeth chattering. "We started taking on water, so I'm guessing we hit a rock underwater or something."

We were on the far side of the bay now, and there were rocks underwater in the shallower areas. Anyone traveling by boat in this area needed to use caution. Nathan was using his sonar to watch for them, but the unexpected still happened.

"Gabriel," Nathan called quickly.

When I glanced his way, he gestured to the cabin below. "We've got towels and dry clothes down there. Can you get everyone down there? Also, two people didn't make it onto the lifeboat. I couldn't see them before, but I'm going to move closer while you get everyone below."

"Got it." I beat feet into the cabin and quickly got everybody situated with towels and dry clothing before hurrying back up to check with Nathan. Considering Nathan and his brothers guided trips for a living, the boat was stocked with enough dry clothing for everyone to change into.

By the time I returned to the deck only moments later, Nathan had gotten close enough for us to see the two remaining passengers. They were clinging to the sinking boat on the far side from where we'd approached. We needed to move fast to get them to safety before gravity took over and pulled the boat underwater. By this point, it was listing heavily to one side.

I glanced at Nathan. "If you can bring the boat over that way"—I gestured to the closest corner where the passengers were clinging to the side—"I think we can probably get the throw ring to them."

Nathan nodded. "Let's do it."

We had no time to waste, and he motored over as quickly as he could without creating a wake to add to the situation. A teenage boy and a young woman were both clearly distressed but staying calm.

"Here's the plan," I called over. "I'm going to toss the ring as close as I can. We need you to do this one at a time. As soon as the throw ring hits the water, jump off, swim to it, and we'll get you on the boat. We have two throw rings, so I'm going to toss them out one after the other. We need to do this quickly, okay?"

The teenage boy called over, "She needs to go first. She's more tired than I am."

The woman opened her mouth to argue, and the teenager shook his head firmly. "I can hang on."

"We're going to try to get both of you at the same time. I'm gonna toss one this way and one the other." I gestured in two directions.

The boy made it quickly to the throw ring, but the woman started to struggle in the water. I called back to Nathan. "I'm gonna dive in and get her." I knew I could handle it with my life vest on.

In seconds, that icy water was numbing, but I swam quickly to reach the woman, circling my arm under her armpits and swimming backward. My lifeguard training from back in high school was serving me well at this moment. Just when we were about to reach the boat, a heavy piece of debris struck my legs, and I couldn't help my loud grunt as I almost lost my hold on the woman.

"Oh, my God! Are you okay?" She gasped.

I didn't know what the hell had hit me, but I knew it had cut me. Even though it was freezing, I could feel the piercing pain on my calf.

I spoke through gritted teeth and continued swimming. "I'll be fine."

With the help of Nathan, another man, and the teenage boy, who was freezing cold but a champ under stress, we were both in the boat only minutes later. Nathan glanced at my leg. "Fuck," he said.

"I know. The cold should help." I rolled up my soaking pants to see a deep gash on the side of my calf just below the knee.

"We can't wait to motor in," he said abruptly.

He'd already radioed in that we had picked up the people from the sinking boat, and we knew a salvage crew would head out tomorrow. But at the moment, there was no rescue crew on the way. We were now a solid two hours from the harbor.

"I'm going to radio in again," he said. "I think it's best if we just sit tight. I'm worried if we try to start, we won't beat the darkness."

I knew he was right, but I wanted to argue the point. Nathan was having none of it and just ignored me after barking out orders. I waited in the cabin below, an emergency blanket wrapped around me after I changed into dry clothing. The cold had set in, though, and my teeth kept chattering.

All I wanted was to talk to Nora, but that wasn't happening. We had zero cell reception out here, not to mention I wasn't thinking clearly.

"When were they supposed to be back?" I asked Flynn with a mixture of anxiety, dread, and cold fear spinning inside my chest. I had hurried over to the resort when Daphne texted, saying I might want to come over and check in with Flynn about Gabriel's trip.

"Over two hours ago," he said, his tone measured.

"Have you called the harbor?" I pressed.

"Of course, I have. I've also been in touch with Jared and Luke. There was a mayday call from a boat nearby, and they went to help with the rescue. Everything went fine, except—" Flynn paused, his eyes searching my face.

I threw my hands up in the air in frustration. "Just tell me!"

"Gabriel got injured in the water when he helped bring in one of the passengers who was struggling. He's going to be fine, and I don't have any more details except everyone is alive."

My stomach took a dive and spun unsteadily. I swallowed and tried to take a deep breath, but it didn't work very well. "When will they get to the harbor?"

"I spoke to Darren at the police station, and he said it should be in about an hour. I'm assuming they'll take Gabriel and the rest of the passengers straight to the hospital."

"Let's go. Now."

"Nora, they're not even—" he began, stopping abruptly when I spun away and started to run out of the resort.

"You're not driving!" he called as he followed me out.

Daphne appeared on the porch beside him a second later, slinging a backpack over her shoulder. "We don't have a guest dinner tonight. It was just staff because Gabriel was going to bring us fresh salmon. Let's all go. We can wait together."

The sun was setting as we hurried off the porch into the parking area. Having lived in Alaska my entire life, I usually found solace in its natural beauty. At the moment, the sky was awash in shades of lavender and deep pink mingled with wispy silver and gold from the late autumn sunset. The snowy mountain peaks were tinted in pink, looking almost otherworldly in the early evening light. Yet the beauty barely registered for me beyond a simple observation. I was too anxious, too tied up with worry over Gabriel and feeling near frantic about putting distance between us. Again.

"Let's take my SUV," Daphne commented as Flynn started to veer toward one of the resort trucks.

His stride shifted, and he followed her over to her SUV.

"Wait!" Cat called.

Glancing over my shoulder, I saw her coming out of the main doors as she tugged on a jacket and ran down the stairs. "I can't believe you guys were going without me." She skidded to a stop beside me as I curled my hand over one of the back door handles.

Before I could reply, Flynn glanced over. "We're in a hurry. Hop in."

Even though I was freaking out more than a little inside, I was relieved to be with my family. My brother's unflappable calm presence was helpful, and Daphne's warm, quiet support was a balm to my jangled nerves.

Daphne moved to get in the driver's seat, but Flynn caught her lightly on the elbow. "I'll drive."

She looked up at him, her eyes narrowing. When she opened her mouth to reply, he shook his head sharply. "Sweetheart, I drive faster than you," he said bluntly.

Daphne immediately handed him the keys and rounded the front of the SUV to climb in the passenger side. As she was buckling up, she replied, "I know you do, and speed is of the essence this time."

As Flynn started driving, I laced my fingers together in an attempt to quell the rising tide of worry, dread, and regret from overwhelming me. It was to no avail. I mentally castigated myself for pulling back and getting upset over something so minor. So what if Gabriel didn't want to talk to me about his mother? Perhaps he felt he'd said all there was to say. It's not as if I enjoyed talking about my father.

At least the first time I broke things off with him, I could make sense of it. This time, my own defensiveness was my only excuse—defensiveness undergirded and made more powerful by fear. I was deeply in love with him and afraid I couldn't have what I wanted with him.

I stared out the window, watching as early evening shifted to twilight while Flynn drove. When I looked ahead once, I saw Daphne reach across the seat and murmur something to Flynn. He caught her hand in his and lifted it to press a kiss on the inside of her wrist.

The moment was brief, lasting no more than seconds, yet the intimacy shimmered between them. It was its own force. My grumpy brother was so in love, and I was so happy for them. I wanted something like that with Gabriel. All of my worries felt small and insignificant now. If he was really hurt, or— It was as if tires screeched in my brain. I couldn't even let myself think about the worst-case scenario.

"Everyone's alive, right?" My question came out in a rush in the quiet space of the vehicle.

My eyes stung with tears, and I knuckled them away. Cat whipped her gaze toward me, her eyes widening as she drew in a sharp breath.

"Of course. I already told you that," Flynn said, his tone calm and level.

"Are you sure?"

"I'm positive."

I fumbled for my phone, abruptly realizing I didn't even have it with me. "Can somebody lend me their phone?" I asked, my voice shaky.

"Let me call," Daphne said from the front as Cat shimmied on the seat to get her phone out of her back pocket.

"Let me—" I began.

Flynn's voice cut through, clear, commanding, and decisive. "Let Daphne call for an update. You're too upset."

For once, I didn't argue with my brother. I'd spent the majority of my childhood proving I was a tough girl. With two older brothers, being tough and independent was a primary goal. I hated being emotional and overwrought, but right now, even *I* knew I probably wouldn't be sensible if I couldn't get the answers I wanted.

Flynn calmly recited the local police's non-emergency number to Daphne before she lifted the phone to her ear. After a moment, she said, "Hello, Darren. We figured we'd try you first. This is Daphne Bell. We were wondering if you had an update on the group on Nathan Winters' boat. I'm with Flynn, Nora, and Cat, and we're on the way to the hospital to check on Gabriel."

She was quiet as she listened, offering a few murmured hums before she finally asked, "When do you think they'll arrive at the hospital?"

Another pause, which felt like forever, before she said, "Got it. We should be there in about fifteen minutes. Please call this number if you have any more updates. Thank you again."

I had no idea how long the conversation actually took. It couldn't have been more than two or three minutes. All the while, though, my heart thudded in a sick beat of dread in my chest, and I had to swallow against the bile rising in my throat. My hands were cold and clammy. I unlaced my fingers and tucked my hands under my thighs to warm them.

Cat unbuckled her seat belt and turned around, leaning over the back seat and rummaging for something. Annoyed with her motion, because my nerves felt strung tight with the air itself chafing on my skin, I asked, "What are you doing, Cat? You need to turn around and buckle up."

Even to my ears, my voice sounded scratchy and irritated.

Cat turned around but then surprised me by carefully placing a soft blanket over my legs.

"You're cold," she explained when I peered over at her.

My heart pinched at her sweetness. "I am. Sorry I got a little snippy there."

"It's okay. Gabriel's gonna be fine. Right, Daphne?" she prompted.

"Everyone's going to be okay. Darren doesn't have any updates from Flynn's earlier call. He thinks they should be in the harbor shortly. The emergency crew said they'll be bringing several of the passengers on the original boat to the hospital for hypothermia and Gabriel to deal with whatever happened to his leg. He's also hypothermic. But that's to be expected, given that he had to dive in the water," she said matter-of-factly.

I tried to take a breath, but it was hard. When I tried again, my throat caught with a sob, and then I burst into tears. Cat scooted closer to me, buckling herself into the middle of the back seat before she curled her arm around my shoulders. "Nora, he's going to be okay. Please don't cry," she pleaded.

I lifted my head, swiping at my tears again. Daphne wordlessly handed back a small packet of tissues. Because, of course, she had tissues with her. She was the kind of person who was always prepared.

I wiped my face and blew my nose while Cat rubbed a palm up and down my back. Talk about role reversal. My seventeen-year-old sister was trying to make me feel better. I felt like a crying hot mess.

"I'm okay," I said between sniffles after several shaky breaths.

When I looked at Cat, the worry in her eyes made my heart clench tightly. "I swear, I'm okay."

"Does this mean you're going to take my advice?" she asked.

If the circumstances were anything other than this, I would've thought she was trying to annoy me. She loved to be right. I recognized that tendency in her because I shared it. Just now, though, I sensed she really wanted to know if I was going to wise up about Gabriel.

I managed a wobbly smile. "Probably."

"What's the advice?" Daphne asked, turning slightly and hooking her elbow on the back of her seat.

"Cat might've told me I was being a little stupid about Gabriel."

Daphne nodded, shifting her eyes to Cat. Cat smiled. "Well, she is." Her eyes bounced to me. "You obviously love him."

My heart gave a hard thump as if in agreement. "How is that obvious?" I blew my nose again.

"Because you never cry and fall apart." Her eyes were worried as she squeezed her arm around my shoulders again.

"Crying and falling apart means I'm in love?" I tried to tease, but it didn't work.

Cat looked at me solemnly, her head bobbing with a nod. "I think so."

Daphne chimed in. "Yes, it does."

Chapter Twenty-Eight

GABRIEL

I was shivering all over, so hard that my teeth kept chattering. My leg throbbed. I tried to cling to some sense of control, but it was eluding me. I was accustomed to being the one who kept my shit together in an emergency. I hated feeling as if my control was slipping through my grasp, and I couldn't stop thinking about Nora.

"Can you let me call her now?" I asked Nathan between rough shivers.

He was climbing into the ambulance where I was, telling the crew he was going to ride with me because he could talk to any family once we got there. He glanced at me. "You don't sound good. I think you're gonna freak her out," he said flatly.

I couldn't even reply when a shiver struck me so hard, my teeth clicked loudly, jarring my jaw with the force. One of the med techs moved to wrap a heated blanket around me. I was wearing an old pair of Nathan's sweatpants and a T-shirt. They'd used an emergency blanket on the boat to keep in my body heat, but the shock of it and the gash on my leg made it difficult to stay warm.

"Th-the o-only ad-ad-advantage wi-with be-be-being this cold means I don't feel the pain as much." I finally managed to get some words out in full by the end of the sentence.

Nathan dipped his chin in acknowledgment. "You're gonna be fine. What a fucking day."

I knew I was in no shape to talk to Nora, but the need to tell her I loved her was a heavy weight. Hell, although I was freezing and in pain, I *needed* to talk to her. I cleared my throat to get Nathan's attention. He looked down at me.

"Please tell Nora I love her."

"Of course," he said.

Happily married to Tess for several years now, Nathan understood love. While we were friends, he didn't know me the way some of my friends did. He probably had no idea how much it meant for me to be in love, but he took my request in stride, and his easy acceptance soothed me.

After that, exhaustion overtook me. I was so tired that I didn't even realize I had fallen asleep, or something like sleep, until I felt the stretcher I was on being moved again. Bright lights blinked above me when I opened my eyes as they wheeled me down the hallway. "I need to see—"

A nurse interjected, "We can't have you see anybody yet, sir. We need to clean that wound on your leg and get a better look at it."

"But—"

A doctor arrived, walking briskly alongside the stretcher as we turned into a room. "Sir, you will be able to see family soon. Based on the EMTs' report, this shouldn't take too long."

They moved efficiently as a team once they got me in an examination room. Before I knew it, the nurse said, "Okay, we're going to give you something to relax you." That was the last thing I remembered.

Chapter Twenty-Nine

NORA

"How much longer will it be?"

The nurse at the desk glanced up with a patient smile. I'd lost count of how many times I'd come up to the circular desk and asked that very question. "He's out of surgery, and everything went well. As soon as he's cleared for visitors, I promise I'll come find you."

Curling my arms around my waist, I murmured, "Thank you."

I was restless, and it was hard to sit in the waiting room. Cat was texting with her friends to pass the time. While Daphne, ever efficient, had somehow remembered to bring her computer tablet and was planning menus for the resort. Flynn seemed content to lounge in a chair flipping through channels on the wall-mounted television.

Nothing was helping me calm my internal state. I felt raw and split open by this event. It wasn't helping to know that Gabriel was okay. I needed to see him, to touch him, to tell him that I'd been stupid. *Again*. I was terrified, and all of it was tangling together in a messy knot in my chest. Unable to shake the restlessness revving through me, I started walking down the hall. The hallways created a giant square around the nursing station. I figured I might as well treat it like exercise.

I'd completed three laps around the grid when I heard someone call, "Hey, Nora!"

Turning, I saw Violet Hamilton walking briskly toward me. She was wearing neon green scrubs with a matching hair tie holding up her glossy dark hair. Her ponytail swung as she approached me in the hallway.

I stopped, offering a simple, "Hey." I couldn't seem to summon more than that.

"What are you doing here?" she asked when she reached me.

"We're waiting for Gabriel. He was in the boat."

Before I even finished speaking, Violet lightly smacked her palm on her forehead. "Of course! He was with Nathan. They're fine. I've already talked to Nathan. He's hanging out in my lab with Sawyer. Come on, you can get the update."

She started to slide her hand through my elbow, but I shook my head. "I want to stay near the nurses' station," I explained when she raised a quizzical brow.

"As soon as we get to the lab, I'll call and tell them to let me know right away when he can have visitors."

She didn't wait and towed me along with her. Violet was a force of nature. I *did* want to talk to Nathan. He had actually seen Gabriel since it happened. Violet was a phlebotomist and the manager at the hospital lab. When we stepped into the lab's waiting area, I saw Nathan Winters sitting on a chair with Sawyer Hamilton, Violet's husband, nearby.

As soon as he noticed me, Nathan straightened. "Gabriel's fine, Nora. I have a message for you."

"What's that?" I asked, trepidation sliding through me.

"Gabriel wanted me to make sure you knew he loved you." Nathan, with his almost black curls and rich blue eyes, looked so earnest when he spoke that a peculiar ache thumped in my heart. He was typically lighthearted and carefree and always quick with a joke. Just now, though, he was somber as he watched me. The next thing I knew, Sawyer stood and grabbed a box of tissues off the table and all but shoved a few into my hands.

Violet curled her arm around my shoulders and squeezed. "Gabriel's going to be okay. I just called over to the nurses' station. They said it shouldn't be long before he's cleared for visitors."

I sniffled and blew my nose. "Why is it taking so long? Did something go wrong?"

Violet shook her head quickly. "No, no. They said he's doing well. I'm sure it won't be long."

I sat down in one of the chairs, slowly glancing amongst them and offering, "I'm sorry. I'm not usually such a mess."

"No need to apologize," Sawyer said with an easy shrug.

At that moment, the sound of footsteps coming down the inner hallway behind Violet's desk reached me. I glanced over to see their young son making his way down the hallway, dragging his fingertips on the wall.

"All done, Mama," he called. "I washed my hands!" He held up his small hands as he entered the waiting area, looking curiously at me and then his parents, a twitch of worry appearing between his brows.

Their son, Alec, probably had no idea why I was sitting in the waiting room crying. Violet knelt beside him, lifting her hand and giving her son a high five. My heart squeezed, almost painfully. Sawyer and Violet were another one of those couples—in love and happy. Every happy couple made me think of Gabriel. I only hoped I hadn't screwed things up too much with him.

"Good job, buddy." When Alec looked back toward me, Violet added, "Nora's okay. Do you remember Gabriel?"

Alec peered over at me, replying, "She's not Gabriel."

I laughed and dabbed at my nose again. "No, I'm not Gabriel. Remember me? I'm Nora. I think I saw you last time at the grocery store."

"She works out at that cool building," Sawyer offered as Alec walked away from his mother over toward his father. Sawyer scooped him onto his lap.

"The octagon!" Alec announced.

"That's the one," I offered with a smile.

Sawyer stood when Alec wiggled on his lap. He crossed to Violet's side as he lowered his son to the floor and held his hand. He leaned down to press a kiss to her temple before he glanced at Nathan and then me. "I'm sure you could use a few minutes to get caught up." Looking back toward Violet, he added, "I'll wait for you outside. Good to see you, Nora."

As soon as Sawyer and Alec had disappeared down the hallway, Nathan looked toward me and asked, "Would you like an update?"

It occurred to me then that he probably hadn't wanted to explain everything that happened in front of a child who would likely have tons of questions.

Violet paused beside me. "I'm closing down for the evening, so you two can chat away. Nobody will be stopping by. I'll hear the phone ring when the nursing station calls. I promise."

She squeezed my shoulder lightly before spinning away and circling behind the desk again. She began tapping away on a laptop while Nathan explained what happened. "Long story short, we responded to a mayday call for a boat taking on water. After we got the majority of the passengers to safety, we had to pull closer because two passengers hadn't made it to the lifeboat. That's when Gabriel dived in to help a woman struggling to reach the throw ring. Some debris struck his leg and cut him."

I absorbed the information and took a breath. "How bad is the cut?"

"He's got a pretty big gash. The EMTs told me they were worried about cleaning it. Then he was freezing after being in the water. It was a series of events that went from not that bad to bordering on hypothermia. But he's fine. I promise. He was really worried about talking to you. I didn't want to call you before because he didn't sound good, and I was concerned it would scare you."

"Scare me? How would that scare me?" I sputtered.

Nathan's smile was gentle. "His teeth were chattering, and he could hardly talk. I figured I would see you here."

I leaned back in the chair, letting out a tattered sigh. It helped to know what had happened, but now I just wanted to make sure Gabriel was okay and warm. What if they weren't checking on that?

"Stop catastrophizing," Violet called from where she was.

I looked over at her. "What do you mean?"

"You've got a look on your face, the kind where you're imagining every single horrible scenario. I promise he's in good hands." Just then, the phone on her desk rang, and she lifted the receiver swiftly.

I leaped from my chair. My knees were so wobbly they gave way, and I plunked down just as Nathan had stood to steady me.

Violet hung up the phone. "Go to the waiting room. The doctor's headed down there to give you all an update."

"I'm walking with you," Nathan announced, curling his hand around my elbow when I stood again.

I hurried down the hallway, feeling shaky and unsettled. I almost plowed an elderly woman over because I wasn't even paying attention. I might've been annoyed at Nathan's offer to walk with me, but it turned out to be a good thing because he pulled me out of the way before I knocked the poor woman to the floor.

"I'm so sorry," I blurted out.

Her eyes blinked in her weathered face as she cast a warm smile, clearly unperturbed. "You're obviously in a rush, so you'd best get there."

Seconds later, I practically skidded into the waiting area to find the doctor, Quinn, standing with Daphne and Flynn. Cat was sitting nearby, leaning forward in her chair as she listened.

"How is he?" I demanded when I stopped beside Quinn.

"Gabriel's stable," he said simply. Quinn's steady presence soothed me. "We'll probably never know what kind of debris slammed into his leg, but it was sharp enough to give him a nice gash. He'll have a scar as a souvenir. Otherwise, he's doing well, and his body temperature has returned to normal. He didn't need anesthesia, but I used a local anesthetic and sedated him while I cleaned and stitched his wound."

I'd known Quinn for years. He ran the family medical clinic in town, and he and his wife also ran a small guiding outfit in Alaska. We occasionally coordinated with them to send customers their way and vice versa.

Quinn smiled at me when all I managed to do was bob my head up and down in response. "He's resting. Let's start with one visitor at a time. I presume you'd like to go first."

I glanced at Flynn, and he nodded. "Of course. Go. We'll wait."

It seemed like everyone considered Gabriel and me a couple, and I wasn't sure how to handle that.

Quinn walked with me to the recovery room, placing his hand on my shoulder at the door. "He's tired, so don't expect him to be functioning at full force. He should be ready to discharge in about an hour or two. The admin team will take care of the paperwork, and Gabriel will need to schedule with me to get the stitches removed."

I nodded impatiently, and then Quinn finally opened the door. I thought he was going to come in with me, but he gave me a light push between my shoulder blades. "Go on in. You can have some privacy."

The sound of the door closing with a whisper and a soft click behind me was unnaturally loud in the quiet room. Gabriel's auburn hair was bright against the white pillows. His eyes were closed as I approached the bed. My pulse tapped out a rapid and unsteady beat when I stopped beside him.

I couldn't resist touching him, reaching for the hand that rested beside his hip. It was warm, and the moment I touched him, his fingers curled around mine. He rolled his head toward me and opened his eyes.

I promptly burst into tears. His eyes widened, and

he moved to sit up, at which point I realized that was a bad thing. I pressed my palm to his chest. "I'm fine," I insisted as I swiped at my tears. "I love you, and I'm sorry I screwed things up again."

When he tried yet again to sit up, I shook my head. "Stop it. You need to rest."

"Sit," he said.

He shifted over, and I slid my hips on the side of the bed, keeping a hold of his hand and pulling it into my lap.

"I'm fine," I repeated. I tried to take a breath and hiccupped instead. "I'm so glad you're okay." My words were a ragged whisper, and my emotions felt stretched beyond their limit. "I thought you were going to die."

"I wasn't even close to dying," he said flatly.

He tugged his hand out of mine and pulled me into his arms. I clumsily shifted to rest against his side and breathe him in. He smelled sterile, almost not like himself. The antiseptic scent overlaid his usual crisp, masculine scent. But it was there underneath, and I buried my head against his neck and took several deep breaths.

I could feel the steady thump of his heart under my palm where it rested on his chest, and a deep sense of relief washed through me.

Gabriel was alive, and he was okay, and that was all I really needed to know.

His palm circled in the center of my back, and he murmured into my hair, "You didn't screw things up. We're fine. We're just not all that great at this."

With a laugh, I sniffled against his neck before lifting my head. His mossy-green gaze was waiting for mine, and the love I saw there snatched my breath out of my lungs.

My laughter faded, and I lifted my hand to smooth one of his brows, explaining, "It was messy."

His lips twitched at the corners, and I felt his fingers sifting through my hair. "Okay." He stared at me somberly for a moment before adding, "I got defensive when you asked about my mom. I get tired of talking about her." He lifted a shoulder in a slight shrug.

"Gabriel, you don't have to talk about this now. I'm sorry I pressured you and then got upset."

"You had a point. I know I love you, but I'm not used to what love means, and I'd rather just say it now. We can talk more later. To clarify, I don't talk about her much because it's an old story. At least to me. You know the basics, but you don't know that the only reason she ever calls me is for money. I find I can't tell her no."

I leaned over and pressed a kiss on the underside of his jaw. Lifting my head again, I said, "No wonder it's frustrating. I'm sorry."

His lips twisted to one side. "It's okay. I've accepted that I can't change the situation, but I think I would hate myself if I didn't help her when she needed it."

"You *really* didn't have to talk about this now," I said softly.

"I know, but I wanted to," he insisted.

I rested my head on his shoulder again, tracing the muscled planes of his chest through the thin sheet. Because it was Gabriel and me, and we were plastered together in a bed, the familiar hum of desire shimmered in the air around us, a light net of sparks. Because it was Gabriel, and he was *that* kind of man, he even tried to make a move on me, sliding his palm down my back, over the curve of my bottom, and giving me a light squeeze.

I rose up on an elbow. "Are you insane? For starters, we're in a hospital, and someone could walk in at any time. Also, not now." I scrambled away, resting my hips on the edge of the bed and keeping my hand curled around his. "You need to rest until you feel better."

He rolled his eyes. "It's just my calf. I can't feel a thing right now."

I couldn't help my smile this time. Tears rolled down my cheeks, and I was laughing as joy was spinning in little pinwheels through my body.

"Any idea when they're gonna let me get the hell out of here?"

"Soon, I hope. Quinn said in an hour or two."

Chapter Thirty

GABRIEL

I leaned back in Nora's bed with a sigh, wincing slightly as I adjusted my leg on a pillow. Nora had insisted I put it under my knee because Quinn said elevation would keep the swelling down.

Nora came walking into the bedroom with two mugs in hand. She was wearing her robe, and her skin was flushed and dewy from a shower. Quinn had reluctantly given me permission to shower as long as I was careful not to get the bandaging over my injury wet.

I wanted to rid myself of the cold, clammy feeling clinging to me from being in the water and the antiseptic smell from the hospital. Nora had insisted on supervising me, and honestly, I hadn't minded it one bit. Being fussed over by her was much nicer than the past few weeks when we'd stumbled out of sync again.

"Tea for me and hot chocolate for you," she explained as she set a mug on the nightstand beside me and rounded the bed.

"For a second, I thought you were going to try to make me drink tea," I teased dryly.

After setting her tea down on the other nightstand, she climbed into bed beside me, tucking the covers over her hips before propping the pillows up behind her. Her lips twitched when she looked in my direction. "I know you hate tea, but I know you love hot chocolate."

"No beer?" I pressed hopefully.

She pursed her lips and narrowed her gaze. "You know Quinn said no alcohol tonight. And if you take pain meds tomorrow, you can't have it then either," she said primly.

I leaned deeper into the pillows and let out a sigh. "It's not like I'm going anywhere, so I don't see why not."

She actually clucked at me before reaching over to push down the covers and check on my leg. "I just want to make sure the bandage isn't damp." Her eyes flicked down as she slid her palm carefully over my thigh and down to check the bandage below my knee. The injury was on the outer edge of my calf. I was grateful whatever the hell had slammed into me hadn't hit me in the knee. I didn't need to be worried about trying to heal and screw up my knee while I was at it.

"You already checked the bandage after I showered," I commented.

"I just want to check again," she insisted.

"Is it still dry?" I teased.

She pursed her lips again when her eyes lifted to mine. "Yes. It is."

Because I was who I was, and apparently, I couldn't be near Nora without wanting her, desire spun like liquid fire through my veins. It didn't matter that her touch wasn't even remotely sexual. She tugged the covers back over my leg, and I caught her hand, pulling her close quickly enough that she rolled against me with a surprised laugh.

"Gabriel! Be careful."

She was half leaning on me, and I could feel the soft press of her breasts. A treacherous tenderness stole through me as I stared into her eyes.

"I missed you," I murmured while I brought her a little closer and dusted my lips across hers.

Sparks flew as if leaping from a bonfire into the air around us. She didn't draw away, not when I teased my tongue along the seam of her lips and tasted her again, savoring the glide of her tongue against mine. I ached for her—body, heart, and soul.

Alas, she ended our kiss all too soon. Lifting her head, she murmured, "Just a kiss. That's all."

I shook my head. "No. I need you tonight." My voice was low and taut, drawn tight with the force of my need for her.

She opened her mouth to protest, shaking her head wildly.

I shook mine in return. "It's my leg. I need you right here," I murmured. Moving swiftly, I tugged her onto my lap, gratified when her knees fell on either side of my hips.

She let out a gasp when she felt the hard ridge of my arousal conveniently nestled under her hot core. When I reached between us, I let out a groan. "You're not wearing panties."

"I just got out of the shower. I don't usually wear underwear under my robe," she said, biting her bottom lip as her cheeks flushed pretty and pink.

Shifting slightly, I teased my fingers into her slick and swollen folds. "Don't try to tell me you don't want me."

I used my free hand to untie her robe, watching it fall open. I immediately leaned forward to catch one of her nipples with my mouth. Her fingers speared into my hair, and she let out a ragged whimper as I gave her nipple a sweet suck.

"Gabriel—" she began again.

I turned my attention to her other nipple. Whatever she meant to say was lost in the moment. I knew if I gave her time to protest, she would scramble off my lap and get all fussy about me. I needed nothing more than to be inside her. In another smooth move, I shifted her back on my lap. The friction of the motion dragged my briefs down with her, and my cock sprang free.

"Come here," I murmured against her lips. When she hesitated, my brain fired off a rational thought. "Oh, right, condom." I moved to reach for the table by the bed, but she shook her head.

"I'm on the pill."

My eyes widened. "Since when?"

"Since before we broke up last time. I was going to tell you, but then—"

"I was a dumbass," I offered helpfully.

She bit her lip, her lashes sweeping down. I nudged my knuckles under her chin, and she lifted her eyes to mine. "I'll still wear a condom if you prefer." We stared at each other, and it felt as if the air was shimmering around us.

She shook her head slowly, all the while my heart was thudding hard in my chest. I pressed a fierce kiss to her lips before I brought her closer and guided her hips down over me.

The sweet tang of her scent surrounded me as I filled her, savoring the silky clench of her channel around me. When she settled down over me, and I was buried deeply, I leaned back, letting my gaze soak her in.

Her dark hair fell in a tousle around her shoulders.

With her robe open, she looked like a goddess in the dim lighting.

My heart beat hard and free in my chest, and a sense of peace stole through me, twining like a vine with my intense desire for her.

"I love you." My words were a promise, clear and strong.

"I love—" Nora gasped when I leaned up and caught her "you" in a kiss.

We rocked together, and I knew she was already chasing her release. The slick fusion of where we were joined created an intense friction as she rippled around me. A slurred groan escaped at the feel of being bare inside her.

Her breath became tattered, and she gasped, "Gabriel, please—"

I teased my fingers over her swollen clit, and a sharp, keening cry escaped when she clamped around my cock, pulling me with her as I came inside her in deep surges.

A moment later, she fell against me, whispering, "I don't want to hurt you."

"I promise you didn't. But if you climb off me now, you'll break my heart."

I felt her giggle against my skin where her head was tucked in the curve of my neck. A little while later, I let her fuss over me some more and then fell asleep, my hot chocolate forgotten.

Gabriel cast me a bemused smile. "It's a little sore, but that's it. I promise you can stop fussing over it."

I rested my hands on my hips and narrowed my eyes. "Are you sure it's not bothering you? You were scratching at it last night when you were asleep."

I rolled my eyes. "It itches because it's getting better," he countered.

I couldn't help but chuckle at the irritated look on his face. "Probably true," I said as I crossed the kitchen to him and leaned down.

I meant my kiss to be brief, but Gabriel slid his hand around the back of my neck, drawing me close and angling my head to the side when he took command. By the time he pulled back, I was breathless, and my pulse was thundering in my ears.

"Now, what time is my appointment with Quinn today?" he asked, a satisfied gleam in his eyes.

I straightened and turned to walk to the counter on slightly unsteady legs. Sweet hell. I couldn't help but wonder just how long it would take me to get used to the effect he had on me. Of course, I thought that effect would've passed already. If anything, it seemed to be getting worse now that the barriers had fallen away between us.

I poured myself a cup of coffee, glancing at him. "Coffee?"

"Always."

I poured two cups, adding a dash of cream to mine and carrying his over. "Not always," I replied as I set his mug down on the table and slipped into the chair across from him. "If it's evening, you want a beer."

He took a swallow, chuckling as he lowered his mug. "Fair enough. So, what time is my appointment?"

"Two. Do you want me to go with you?"

He eyed me for a few beats. "Maybe," he said cautiously. "But not if you're going to lecture me in front of Quinn."

"I won't lecture you. I'll just make sure that we know what his recommendations are so you don't screw up your recovery."

Gabriel took a long swallow of coffee, his gaze speculative. "Nora, it's a cut. That's it, just a cut."

"A paper cut is technically just a cut," I replied tightly. "That gash was no minor cut. It required deep cleaning and stitches."

His gaze softened, and he reached across the table, catching my hand in his. "Babe, I needed stitches, and they had to clean it, but that's it. I know it's worse than a paper cut, but I'm really fine."

Suddenly, tears pressed hot at the backs of my eyes. "I know," I said thickly. "But it scared me."

"I know. I love you. You can fuss over me all you want."

I smiled through my blurry gaze. "Okay," I whispered.

At that moment, his phone vibrated on the table. He released my hand and spun it around to glance at the screen. "It's my mom," he offered, his eyes lifting to mine.

"Go ahead and take it. Unless you'd rather not."

"I'll take it. It's easier to deal with it right off."

He lifted the phone to his ear as he dragged his thumb across the screen. "Hey, Mom, what's up?"

I couldn't hear what she was saying, but I heard the murmured sounds of a voice as he nodded. "Doing fine. How are you?"

A few more murmurs, and then he nodded and said, "I'll take care of it. Don't worry."

He nodded along to whatever she said, before replying, "Take care, Mom. I'll talk to you later." He hung up the phone and set it down. I waited, nursing my coffee and not wanting to press.

"She needed some money. That's usually what she calls for."

"Do you mind?" I asked carefully, hoping I didn't unintentionally slam the door shut on this opening between us.

He shrugged. "Not really. She never asks for much, and I have it. Mostly all I do is save the money I earn here."

"You don't mind even though she wasn't there for you when you were growing up?"

He shook his head. "No. Like I told you, I'd feel worse if I didn't. I didn't understand it when I was younger, but she didn't have what she needed, and she was an alcoholic. She's sober now, at least as far as I know. Maybe she couldn't be there for me when I was a kid, but I'd regret not helping her. It's not a big deal. That's actually easier to give her than if she suddenly wanted to be a big part of my life."

"You're a good man, Gabriel," I said softly, once again feeling the hot press of tears in my eyes.

Because he *was* a genuinely good man. I loved him, and he loved me, and I would never again carelessly let my defenses discard the heart he'd given to me to protect. I'd cherish it for the rest of my life.

His lips quirked slightly at the corners before worry chased through his eyes. "Are you crying?" He reached over, catching my fingers in his and rubbing his thumb over the back of my hand.

"I'm just emotional. That's all." I took a breath. "How does your sister feel about your mom?"

"She's a little more bitter than me." He wrinkled his nose at that. "And that's okay. She and I stay in touch, and we're good. I don't think she'd want me to tell Mom to fuck off and not take care of her. But she'd rather not be involved, and that's fine."

"You're a good man," I repeated.

He shifted his chair, scooting around the table to be closer to me. He tugged my chair to face him, his knees bracketing mine as he palmed my cheek. "And you're a good woman, Nora. I love you."

My pulse tapped wildly, almost as if it were clapping. "I love you too."

His forehead fell to mine, and he gave me a lingering kiss. When he leaned back, he said, "Come with me to that appointment. I'll get my stitches out, and then we can get something to eat in town."

I was laughing, and my heart felt so full it almost ached.

EPILOGUE

Nora

Three years later

I walked into the kitchen at the resort. Correction: I *waddled* into the kitchen at the resort.

Daphne was standing at the counter, chopping onions. I stopped beside her. As soon as the momentum from walking ended, I needed something to hold me up. Turning, I rested my hips against the counter and curled my hands around the edge.

"You okay?" she asked.

"How come you're not as gigantic as me?" I muttered.

She looked over at me and then down at her own round belly. "Because you're due a month before me." She smiled warmly, a glint of sympathy in her eyes.

I rubbed my belly. "Pregnancy isn't fun."

Her head bobbed in agreement. "My first pregnancy was way worse. This one's been easier for me."

Daphne somehow managed to look tidy and prim even though she was six months pregnant to my seven.

I felt like a giant whale, except whales were more graceful than me. Although maybe that was because they were in the ocean, and the water helped. If I could float in a pool for the rest of my pregnancy, I'd be happy to try it.

At the sound of footsteps, I glanced over to the archway between the living room and the kitchen. The second I saw my husband walking through, my lips curled in a tired smile.

Gabriel crossed the room, stopping in front of me and resting his hands beside mine on the counter. "How are you feeling?"

"Tired and my back hurts."

"You look beautiful," he murmured as he dipped his head and pressed a lingering kiss on the side of my neck.

Even though I felt like shit, a kiss from Gabriel in that sensitive area could still send a hot shiver through my entire body.

"Why are you on your feet?" he asked as he drew away, his concerned gaze skating over my face as his arm encircled my waist and lightly rubbed my lower back.

"I don't know," I muttered. "Daphne is on her feet."

Daphne cast me a dry look, her brows hitching up. "For no more than twenty minutes at a time. You've been busy all day. Go sit down. I do half my work in the kitchen sitting on a stool."

Gabriel didn't give me much choice in the matter before he nudged me gently but firmly in the direction of the kitchen table. As soon as I sat down, he pulled another chair over for me to prop my feet on. I wasn't accustomed to letting anyone fuss over me, and I wrestled with conflicted feelings about it. He had been solicitous throughout my pregnancy. A part of me savored it while another part bristled against it. That was my tomboy side, the side with two older brothers who never wanted to be seen as needing anyone's help.

Later that night, we were back home. My house had become our house. Gabriel was finishing up an addition because we needed the space. He had added a new section to the back, so now the upstairs had two bedrooms in addition to a large master bedroom with its own bath and a nursery off to the side.

I was propped up on the pillows in bed, and we were watching a movie. He rolled to the side, sliding his hand over my round belly in a caress. "How are you feeling?"

I slid my eyes sideways. "You just asked me that ten minutes ago. I'm still fine." My lips curved in a smile.

"Never hurts to ask again," he murmured, dusting kisses along the side of my neck before his head rested in the curve of my shoulder.

"We can do this, right?" I asked.

"Absolutely." He lifted his head, his gaze catching mine, radiating confidence and purpose.

Sometimes I didn't know what to do with the man he'd become. After the fraught struggle we'd both gone through trying to accept that loving someone was even possible, we'd settled into a comfortable relationship, the fiery desire that had brought us together still burning.

He'd even reached out to his mom to finally address her pattern of asking for money. While he knew she wouldn't likely ever be all that stable, he'd had that difficult conversation and settled on a plan to send her money on his own because he didn't want her in dire straits. It wasn't a perfect solution, but the lingering tension around her was gone for him, and she only called now to check in.

We sparred occasionally, but it was never difficult to make up. And, oddly for a man who thought he could never be committed, he had an easy confidence about starting a family. I'd watched him be a doting unofficial uncle to Elias and Cammi's twins. He was the one who first brought up trying to get pregnant. Just now, tears pricked in my eyes as I looked into his. "Okay, thanks for the reminder," I whispered.

I fell asleep on my side with him curled behind me and his hand resting on my massive belly. So many things I never expected, and so many things I savored every moment of every day.

GABRIEL

Six months later

It was dark, and a subtle noise filtered through the haze of sleep. I came abruptly awake. Nora was warm and curled up against me. I blinked and glanced around before realizing I was hearing our daughter, Laney. She wasn't crying; she was laughing.

I rolled away from Nora, swinging my legs off the bed. The hardwood floor was cool under my feet as I took the three strides from the bed to where our daughter's crib was against the wall. When I lifted her, she made a little giggling sound and wiggled. I did a quick diaper change on the changing table immediately by the crib.

I slipped back into bed, propping the pillows

against the headboard so I could hold her comfortably. I knew what was coming. I might not've been a father all that long, but I knew she wanted to nurse and would get irritable any second now.

As if on cue, she let out a disgruntled sound, something between a snort and a cry. Nora rose swiftly, moving to climb out of bed before I caught her by the shoulder. "I've got her already," I whispered in the darkness.

Nora turned toward us, a sleepy smile curling her lips. Although the room was mostly dark, we had two night-lights, so I could see a hint of her smile in those glimmers of light.

"Hand her over," she mumbled. She shifted the covers on her lap and propped the pillows behind her.

I carefully passed the small bundle of our daughter over, and a moment later, our baby was nursing. Nora leaned back, rolling her head to the side to look at me. "Thanks for getting her out of her crib," she whispered.

"That's my job," I said, entirely serious.

Nora giggled softly, and the sound was a silk lasso cinching tighter around my heart.

Now that we'd been together for more than a few years, every so often, it was startling for me to contemplate that there'd been a time when I believed I wasn't cut out for love or commitment.

Now? I couldn't imagine life without Nora. Every day was another stitch in the fabric of our shared life and family. That world extended far beyond just the two of us and our daughter, the stitches encompassing our friends and more.

Even with sleep elusive now that we had a baby, I would take every bleary, tired morning as long as I could have it with Nora and our daughter. I shifted closer to them, sliding my arm over Nora's shoulders to sift my fingers through her hair while she nursed. She eventually fell asleep after Laney finished nursing, while I waited a few more minutes before carefully returning our baby girl to her crib.

The next morning, I woke up to find myself alone in bed. Because I didn't want to miss a second of our life, I hurried into the shower and then down to the kitchen, maybe five minutes later.

Nora was standing by the counter with Laney in her arms. "We beat him this morning," she whispered as she pressed a kiss to Laney's cheek and glanced over at me with a bright smile. "I already have coffee ready."

I chuckled and stopped in front of them, resting my hands on either side of them on the counter, encompassing my small family in the cage of my arms. "Good morning," I murmured.

Nora gave me a lingering kiss before I lifted my head and curved my palm over the downy soft hair of our baby girl. She had Nora's big brown eyes paired with wispy locks of auburn hair.

"What are we doing today?" Nora asked when I looked back toward her.

Our daughter gargled and squeaked as if answering.

"I don't know what you're doing, but I'm hanging out with you. Remember? No flights for either one of us today."

The curve of her smile deepened on her cheek. "Oh, that's right. We promised ourselves a day of nothing."

"It's never nothing."

"What do you mean?" she asked when I stepped away to reach for the mug she'd placed beside the coffee maker on the counter.

"I just like hanging out with you, and that's not nothing."

Nora's smile was bright as I circled my arms around her again, abandoning the coffee. When I accidentally squished our baby girl, and she let out a sound of protest, our heads peered to look at her together.

This morning couldn't be any more perfect. It hadn't just been about getting back to us. It was so much more.

Thank you for reading Back To Us - I hope you loved Nora & Gabriel's story!

Up next is Wild With You - a brand new hotshot firefighter series set in the wilds of Alaska!

Graham is a grumpy hotshot firefighter and a single father with a teenage daughter. He does *not* have time for, well, anything.

He was never supposed to see the gorgeous stranger who asked for a kiss ever again. Then, prissy Madison turns out to be his new neighbor. She's a *major* complication for a man who doesn't have time (see above).

He thinks he can keep his hands off of her. He thinks he has control. Spoiler alert: he can't, and he doesn't. Cue the complications.

Is there anything better than a broody, alpha hotshot firefighter who makes a habit of rescuing anyone in need getting brought to his knees by a smart, sassy city-girl completely out of her element?

Don't miss Graham & Madison's smoking' hot, opposites attract romance!

Pre-order Wild With You - due out Aug 31, 2021!

For more swoon-worthy small town romance...

This Crazy Love kicks off the Swoon Series - small town southern romance with enough heat to melt you! Jackson & Shay's story is epic - swoon-worthy & intensely emotional. Jackson just happens to be Shay's brother's best friend. He's also *seriously* easy on the eyes. Shay has a past, the kind of past she would most definitely like to forget. Past or not, Jackson is about to rock her world. Don't miss their story! Free on all retailers!

Burn For Me is a second chance romance for the ages. Sexy firefighters? Check. Rugged men? Check. Wrapped up together? Check. Brave the fire in this hot, small-town romance. Amelia & Cade were high school sweethearts & then it all fell apart. When they cross paths again, it's epic - don't miss Cade's story! Free on all retailers!

For more small town romance, take a visit to Last Frontier Lodge in Diamond Creek. A sexy, alpha SEAL meets his match with a brainy heroine in Take Me Home. Marley is all brains & Gage is all brawn. Sparks fly when their worlds collide. Don't miss Gage & Marley's story!
Free on all retailers!

If sports romance lights your spark, check out The Play. Liam is a British footballer who falls for Olivia, his doctor. A twist of forbidden heats up this swoon-worthy & laugh-out-loud romance. Don't miss Liam & Olivia's story.
Free on all retailers!

Sign up for my newsletter, so you can receive information about upcoming new releases & receive a FREE copy of one of my books: http://jhcroixauthor.com/subscribe/

Dare With Me Series

Crash Into You

Evers & Afters

Come To Me

Back To Us

Light My Fire Series

Wild With You - coming August 2021!

Hold Me Now - coming October 2021!

Only Ever Us - coming December 2021!

Fall For Me - coming February 2022!

Swoon Series

This Crazy Love

Wait For Me

Break My Fall

Truly Madly Mine

Still Go Crazy

If We Dare

Steal My Heart

Into The Fire Series

Burn For Me

Slow Burn

Burn So Bad

Hot Mess

Burn So Good

Sweet Fire

Play With Fire

Melt With You

Burn For You

Crash & Burn

That Snowy Night

Brit Boys Sports Romance

The Play

Big Win

Out Of Bounds

Play Me

Naughty Wish

Diamond Creek Alaska Novels

When Love Comes

Follow Love

Love Unbroken

Love Untamed

Tumble Into Love

Christmas Nights

Last Frontier Lodge Novels

Take Me Home

Love at Last

Just This Once

Falling Fast

Stay With Me

When We Fall

Hold Me Close

Crazy For You

Just Us

ACKNOWLEDGMENTS

Much gratitude to my assistant, Erin, for keeping me on track and for being awesome in general. Thank you to my editor for helping me give Nora & Gabriel the happily-ever-after they deserved and to Terri D. for cleaning up the details. Najla Qamber creates gorgeous covers for me and is so patient with my questions.

A bow of thanks to my early readers who catch any last errors and to the bloggers who spread the word about my stories and so much more.

Gracious thanks to my readers near and far who cheer on my stories, ask when the next one is coming, and send me messages about stories they love - thank you, thank you, thank you.

As always, lots of love to my husband and my dogs for being there.

xoxo

J.H. Croix